LOOK BACK TO YESTERDAY

Keep looking forward!

- Tara Lynn Marta

Look Back to Yesterday

A novel

by

TARA LYNN MARTA

BOOKS

Adelaide Books
New York / Lisbon
2020

LOOK BACK TO YESTERDAY
A novel
By Tara Lynn Marta

Copyright © by Tara Lynn Marta
Cover design © 2020 Adelaide Books

Published by Adelaide Books, New York / Lisbon
adelaidebooks.org
Editor-in-Chief
Stevan V. Nikolic

For any information, please address Adelaide Books
at info@adelaidebooks.org
or write to:
Adelaide Books
244 Fifth Ave. Suite D27
New York, NY, 10001

ISBN: 978-1-952570-50-6

Printed in the United States of America

This book is dedicated to the memory of my mother and father who always encouraged me to follow my dreams.

Contents

Forward

Some people don't believe the past exists, but it does. I've been there and so have you. If you have ever lost someone close and could not move on, then you've been there.

There was a time when the past hounded me, or I hounded the past, however you want to look at it. I was quite stubborn back then, at least that's what the stranger told me after meeting him on a bus to New York.

We had a rocky relationship, me and the stranger. He told me that the past is a wonderful place to visit, but when it prevents you from moving on that's when you become imprisoned by it.

By the way, the trip to which I refer took place when I was thirty-three, about a month and a half after my father died and two weeks after I broke up with my boyfriend John.

Things didn't go as planned. They never do when you live in the past.

The stranger accompanied me on my trip, insisting that I was holding the past and everyone in it hostage. He pushed until I was ready to take back my life. That's what strangers do. They nudge and push and persuade until we yield.

Not everyone sees their stranger. But if you're quiet, you can hear him. Or her.

One

"No man ever steps into the same river twice, for it's not the same river, and he's not the same man."

–Heraclitus

The train barreled down the tracks of a darkened tunnel. I clung desperately to the stanchions as if at any moment I would be hurled through the doors. Flickering lights made it impossible for my eyes to adjust to the subway signs rushing by: DeKalb Avenue. Prospect Park. Avenue M. Kings Highway.

Was I alone on the train? No. I spied shadows at the other end of the subway car.

The train came to a screeching halt. Each set of doors flung open, and the shadows passed through them, one by one, their faces obscured until a shadowy figure took shape. A robust figure with short hair and deep cinnamon eyes materialized. My mother.

I moved in her direction as she exited, but the doors slammed shut, locking me in. I tugged and pulled but they would not budge. I scratched and pounded and screamed:

"Mom, please, don't go!"

Ever since the summer my mother surrendered to cancer when I was nine, I chased her in my sleep. My father would hear me calling for her through the walls of my bedroom. The dreams were always vivid in the morning, but not the cries for her return.

During my first year of junior high, my father touched base with the guidance counselor, Mrs. Krauss. He thought I needed help working through my feelings. She would ask questions and I would stare at the clock, counting the minutes until our session ended.

"How do you feel today, Rebecca?" she'd ask.

How does any kid feel after their mother abandons them?

I pleaded with my father not to make me see Mrs. Krauss anymore, but he said I needed to deal with my grief. So I saw her and another woman from the Community Counseling Center twice a week. But I paid them no mind because being motherless is not a problem.

And then came another brilliant idea.

"Let's take the bus to Brooklyn," Dad said when I was thirteen, then fourteen, then fifteen and sixteen, until he gave up.

I was born in Brooklyn where I lived until my mother died in nineteen eighty-five. We lived downstairs from my grandmother, Flo. But times were hard not to mention expensive. "We can't afford to live here anymore, Becky," said my father. He was surprised at how well I took the news. My grandmother retired to Florida and my father took me to a small town in Pennsylvania.

It was Mrs. Krauss who'd advised Dad that a trip to my hometown might do me well, help me to transition into adulthood better, as she put it.

"I'm not going," I'd chant whenever my father brought it up. "Take that sourpuss guidance counselor if you want to go."

She was into my whole life, Mrs. Krauss, based on whatever my father reported to her. I never said a word. "Want to tell me about your dreams?" she asked during one session.

A more astute person would have taken the hint and dropped the subject. She waited for a response while I picked at the lint on my sweater and flicked it toward her face.

"Dreams can be confusing," she went on. "They can occur due to unresolved pain." She talked and I sat. She paced her office and I sat. "What do you think your dreams are trying to tell you, Rebecca?"

What are dreams anyway? They're scenes in the mind when the body is asleep, and they come in flashes or drag on like a bad play. Sometimes they have a theme. A message. Some people swear they never dream, but we all do. The lucky ones just don't remember.

At thirty-three I was still haunted by dreams of my mother, but chasing her on the subway was new. Unable to fall back to sleep, I went into the bathroom and splashed cold water on my face. I caught a glimpse of myself in the mirror. My petite frame had expanded. At 4 ft. 11, I couldn't afford the extra heft, but the damage had been done.

Maybe that's why John lost interest in me?

My relationship with John lasted longer than I'd expected. But after my father's death, John's eyes and hands wandered.

It was my idea to break off the relationship after I spotted John through the window of La Bella's Italian Cuisine with his co-worker, Heather. He was stroking her cheek with one hand, while his other hand worked its way through her long blond hair. I struck the window with my house keys and John jumped to his feet, fluttering his hands.

He showed up at my apartment two hours later and rather than apologize, he deposited the blame on me. I didn't pay attention to him anymore. He felt unloved, unwanted. And while he delivered one excuse after another, I told him to get out of my life.

"I want to be alone," I barked as John fled in his BMW. But the words were like razor blades to my soul. I didn't want to be alone. I wasn't good at it.

Leaving John was the right decision. Something always told me so. But in the quiet of the night while the world slept, I'd lie in bed dwelling on the years John and I had shared. It wasn't all bad, even when it was. And when I could no longer silence my thoughts, emails went out: "John, I'm sorry. Let's work things out." And he'd reply, "It's over, move on."

From the bathroom, I went into the kitchen to grab something to eat. The light in the refrigerator was out again. "Do they make anything that lasts anymore?" I sighed.

I hadn't prepared meals in weeks, choosing instead to order takeout, which explained my weight gain. I opened the crisper and retrieved three slices of bologna, all had a slimy texture. I grabbed the mayonnaise and slammed the refrigerator door. Luckily, the bread hadn't molded, so I grabbed two slices and shoved them into the toaster. Once the bread popped out I slathered on the mayo, then added an even layer of bologna.

On the floor in the living room I spread out my feast and turned on the television. With my back against the couch, my mind wandered to my childhood in Brooklyn when Sadie used to babysit me. She always gave me a bologna sandwich for lunch.

It'd been too long since my days in Brooklyn, but the memories brought comfort.

Just thinking about the past wasn't enough. I needed to see it, so I took out the home movies my father had taken. Dad had the movie reels transferred to VHS, until I had them updated to DVD.

Outside shots were more visible, but the ones indoors had faded. How I longed to see the warmth in my family's smiles, as if they were standing right in front of me. Still, I recognized my mother with her short black hair and dark eyes, smiling at the camera, while my grandmother sat sideways on the couch, one leg tucked in, the other stretched across the blue upholstery. My Aunts Elizabeth and Bernice were seated at the dining room table having coffee with Uncle Albert.

Missing was my father who preferred being behind the camera. On rare occasions when he allowed himself to be filmed he stood with his arms at his sides, dressed in a white t-shirt and jeans. Close-ups of his face captured his mustache and sideburns, and his thick brown hair that he kept parted to the side.

Death had claimed those who should have gone on forever. With my family gone, my past consisted of images on a screen. It wasn't enough. But it was all I had.

When John and I were still together, I'd make him watch the films with me, and he would pretend to take interest even though he'd grown bored with my past.

"How old are you in this one?" John asked one night.

"Four maybe."

"Do you remember anything?"

I'd watched my childhood play out on the screen so many times I couldn't tell. "I think so, yeah. My memories start in 1980."

John laughed at a shot of my mother pursing her lips and turning from the camera. "She looks mad at your dad."

"She wasn't mad at my father."

"How do you know?"

"Because my parents never got mad at each other. They were happy. "

"Nobody's parents are happy all the time." John had a way of ruining memories.

"Well, mine were."

"So they never had any problems?" John inquired.

"Nope."

"You know, Becky, there's a lot you don't see when you're young. I mean, you see it, but you can't make sense of it."

"John, I was there. They were happy. Now can we drop it?"

He shoved a fistful of popcorn into his mouth while doing his best to sound coherent. "Why don't you ever visit Brooklyn?"

I offered no answer because I favored the Brooklyn in the home movies more. It never changed.

By the end of the DVD, loneliness set in. I thought about John and how much I missed having him by my side. Though he had not been faithful, he was better than nothing.

Mere thoughts triggered my need to call him. I knew in my heart it would make look weak, pathetic even.

"What do you want, Becky?" he said, answering on the fifth ring.

I swallowed hard after hearing the agitation in his voice. "Do you have a minute?"

"Not right now," he replied. I heard giggling in the background. *Heather.*

"Can I see you tomorrow? I think we should talk."

There was a pause. "Becky, I don't think that's a good idea."

"After all our time together you can't give me five minutes?" I shouted into the phone.

"Rebecca, did you call just to fight?" John used my full name whenever I hit a nerve.

"I just want to talk, John. Is that too much to ask?"

"There's nothing to talk about. You dumped me, remember?"

"Yeah, after you hooked up with that disgusting excuse for a woman."

Then came John's soliloquy about how bankrupt our relationship had been. "You don't get it, do you? Everything in your life revolves around the past, Rebecca."

"You weren't perfect either," I answered. "It takes two to make a relationship work."

"Add to that," John said, "the fact that for a whole year you were distracted by other things."

"I was taking care of my father, John. I'm sorry if I couldn't coddle you all the time. It's not like I had any help from you."

"Your father hated me. I didn't think he'd want me around."

"Any excuse is better than none," I laughed, reiterating a phrase my father had often used.

"So he didn't hate me?" John asked.

"Yes, he hated you. But you could have been more patient?"

"Becky, it wasn't just your father and you know it."

"Tell me doctor, what was it then?"

"It's like you're stuck in childhood. The way you find comfort talking about things you did as a kid, like it brings you back there or something."

The phone crackled as my hand tightened around it. "Don't talk about what you don't understand."

"Nobody is that attached to their parents, Becky." John did not understand loss. He'd never lost a grandparent, never mind a parent. Since we began dating he'd been coddled. Surprise parties, dinners, brunches. He didn't even take vacations without his parents tagging along.

"Says the mama's boy whose mother does everything but breastfeed him."

My cell phone sailed through the living room, connecting with a small clock given to me by my Aunt Elizabeth before her death. But John had incited in me a fury and the fragmented clock would tick no more.

From the moment they'd met my father disliked John. He called him shady, among other things.

"He's a moron," Dad said one afternoon while we lunched at Kentucky Fried Chicken.

"You just have to get to know him better," I replied.

But my father rolled his eyes and slathered gravy on a biscuit.

"You should want better for yourself."

Dad was right. John spent more time with his friends than he did with me. But I hung on, something that irritated my father.

"Well, I can't leave him."

"There's something more to it," he said as he ripped into an extra crispy chicken leg.

"This has nothing to do with Mom if that's where you're going."

"It has everything to do with your mother, Becky. I've watched you struggle with loss from the moment she died."

I threw my hands up and said, "There is nothing I can do about it, OK?"

"You can learn to let go."

"Pretend that my mother never existed?"

Dad put down his chicken leg. "No, stop pretending that she still does."

I inserted the DVD in a plastic case. Inside my bedroom, I searched my dresser drawer for the key to the security box hidden in my closet. Paranoid that my apartment would catch fire and the memories of my family would be destroyed, I kept the DVD, along with other valuables, in a fireproof box.

Before closing the box, I removed a ring from my finger and put it away for the night. The 18K gold diamond initial had been a gift from my father to my mother on her birthday.

My mother bequeathed the ring to me, but Dad didn't let me have it until my senior year of high school. I wore it for the first time at graduation. I looked out into the audience at all the happy mothers, smiling and waving at their sons and daughters. Then I looked down at the ring. What a poor alternative for a proud mother.

I ran a washrag under the facet and moved it across my body. Sitting on the edge of the tub, I ruminated on the endless maze that had become my life. With no schedule to keep it was difficult to tell one day from the next. My job at the attorney's office had ended after my bosses decided that my work was no longer effective. "Please, you can't fire me," I cried. Actual tears. Attorneys have never been known for their sympathy. They dismissed me with a week's severance.

Donning a fresh pair of pajamas I climbed into bed and found refuge in a book. *The Professor's House* by Willa Cather was a favorite that I'd read at least a dozen times. The tattered pages told no lies, and the sheets of paper that were once fastened fell aimlessly onto the bed. I gathered the loose pages in my hands and placed them in their rightful order.

On the tall dresser I scanned a photograph of me and my parents. I must have been around five or six, draped in red pajamas and huddled in my mother's arms. Her head sloped sideways, a slight grin around her mouth. Beside us, my father, his right hand on my back, offering his usual bashful smirk.

I hopped out of bed for a closer look, and then tightened my jaw as I stared into my baby blue eyes. Hidden behind that childish grin lied the suspicion that my mother was not long for this world.

The fear was real and I sensed it – always.

Two

Light blanketed my room. Warm rays radiated my face, inducing me to shelter my eyes against the sun's incessant glow. I did not want the day to begin, but the sparrows outside my window chirped in celebration.

I washed and dressed, opened my closet and got out the ring.

My stomach released a forceful snarl, leading me into the kitchen where the empty cupboards indicated that I was in dire need of a food haul.

Quintero's Market was five blocks from my house, so I procured my father's portable shopping cart – wagon was the term in Brooklyn - and headed out.

Inside Quintero's, shoppers scurried about, snatching bread and milk as if a massive snowstorm was about to hit.

Twice I stopped to kick one of the wheels on the wagon after it jammed. I raced down every aisle for the essentials: boxed macaroni and cheese, frozen pancakes, a six-pack of diet soda, and a chocolate bar to dip in peanut butter.

The checkout lines were a mile long. Thank God for tabloids which kept consumers up to speed on the latest gossip in the lives of celebrities – real or imagined.

A close-up of Elvis splashed across one rag bore the head-line: "Elvis is Still Alive." Consolation to fans who swore they saw him driving around Memphis or up in the window at Graceland. At the time, I didn't make the connection between thousands of groupies who thirsted for Elvis' resurrection and my own desperate need to revive my family.

After paying for my groceries, I left Quintero's with my wagon dragging behind. Its wheels bounced off cracks in the sidewalk, tossing the contents like balls in a bingo cage.

Across from the stucco building where I lived, a mother held her young daughter's hand as the little girl played hopscotch. I marveled at their relationship. Then I drew up one leg and used the other to hop in unison with the girl.

The mother let go of her daughter's hand and a warm flush circulated my body, causing me to stop in my tracks. She should have held onto her child's hand just a bit longer. Children need guidance from a mother, support so they can safely reach adulthood. The little girl didn't understand what it meant for her mother to let go.

But I did.

I jerked the house key from my pocket with unnecessary force, propelling it into a small puddle. As I bent over to re-trieve the key, a twinkle of gold slithered down my finger. My mother's ring rolled a few inches down the pavement, off the curb, then disappeared into a sewer.

I sank to my knees, seized the drain with both hands, and pulled violently on the bars like a prisoner trying to escape their cell. The ring was gone.

Both fists banged the pavement rendering my white knuckles raw. "How could I lose my mother's ring?" I cried.

But no one cared; not the people watering their lawns nor the ones passing by.

A mama bird and two of her babies landed in a nearby puddle. They splashed in the water untroubled. I watched as they shook their feathers and was somewhat comforted by their company. Then the mama bird spread her wings and took flight without her children. They splashed again, unmindful that they were alone, too engrossed in their playfulness to care. "She's gone," I told them. "Your mother left, don't you understand?"

But the birds paid me no mind, so I took my grief and escaped inside my apartment.

Three

Propped in a chair, I lifted my feet to the windowsill. My fingers found their way to my cell phone and dialed my friend Jen's number.

"Jen, this is Becky. Can you please give me a call?" My voice trembled as I left a voicemail for my *former* best friend. The word former is deliberate because we'd gone our separate ways, through no fault of my own.

We had known one another since the sixth grade, both of us quiet and awkward, yet social enough to exchange hellos. She was the first person I confided in about my mother.

"What's your mom like?" she asked during the second week of school."

"I don't have a mother," I answered, squirming.

"Everyone has a mother."

I shrugged and dropped my head.

"My mother's d. . ." But the word wouldn't come.

"Oh, I'm sorry," Jen said when she figured it out. "I never knew a kid whose mother died."

Funny, I'd never thought it was possible for mothers to die, either.

The best part about our friendship was spending time with her mother, who would sometimes invite me to lunch with them.

"God, she never stops talking," Jen complained when her mom went to the restroom during one such lunch.

"I don't mind."

"How can you stand listening to her boring stories?" Jen moaned. "And didn't you just love the lecture on the menstrual cycle?"

"I bet you and your mom do a lot together like shopping and stuff?"

Jen curled her upper lip. "Ugh, yeah. I hate when she takes me shopping."

Her comment came across cold and ungrateful. I thought of myself in Jen's place, shopping and lunching with her mother.

Dad had offered to take me shopping before the start of every school year. He had little fashion sense, so I'd take the bus to the mall alone, doing my best to match shirts with slacks. I'd notice other girls with their mothers, and I'd hide behind racks of clothes to study them. It all seemed so simple, so meant to be. Mothers and daughters shopping. I would mentally trade places with the girls in the store, trying to imagine what it was like to be someone other than an observer. Trying to imagine what it felt like to be a mother's daughter, rather than a motherless daughter.

My friendship with Jen stayed strong while she was single. Enter Kyle. I saw her every few months if I was lucky. It wasn't enough. When she and Kyle married, our friendship became an acquaintanceship.

An hour went by before a light rap at the door. I hadn't the strength to open it.

"The door was unlocked so I just let myself in," Jen said as she strolled through the living room.

I continued to focus on the obscurity beyond the window.

Jen stood at my side, peering in the same direction. "What are you looking at?"

"I was just looking for yesterday."

"As if," she bellowed. Her sharp voice went right through me.

"What do you need?"

"Um, you called me, remember? What did *you* need?"

I wanted our close friendship to resume. Phone calls, lunches, dinners. We had been sidekicks. She had changed even when I wasn't ready.

"You know what," I answered, shifting my body away from her, "forget I called. It wasn't important."

I returned my attention to the window until Jen pulled the cord on the Venetian blinds.

"Becky, your call sounded urgent, so what's wrong?"

"I lost my mother's ring. It fell off my finger and rolled down the sewer." My eyes moistened, but I willed myself not to cry.

"I'm sorry, Becky," she answered as the gold necklace with the heart pendant belonging to her grandmother – who was still living – dangled from her neck.

"I just feel like a part of me is missing now."

"A ring won't bring her back."

I rose from my chair like a gust of wind. Looking straight into Jen's pupils, I shouted, "How would you feel if your precious wedding ring was gone, huh?"

"I'm not saying it wasn't important, Becky. But you act like…"

"Like what?" I implored while my right foot drummed the carpet.

Jen struggled for the words. "Like a ring keeps your mother alive or something."

"That's ridiculous."

"You need to keep busy, Becky, and keep your mind off this stuff."

"I've been trying to find another job, OK?"

"What about going to college?"

"College?" I answered with sarcasm. "What is that the new therapy?"

Once Jen was married her college degree, much like our friendship, was useless.

"Well, if you did go to college, what would you major in?" she queried.

"Something to do with writing."

Jen's lips bent into a smirk. "Like you're going to make a living as a writer!" She sat on the arm of my couch, examining her fingernails like they needed a manicure.

It was my turn to hit back. "I'm sorry, what do you use your degree for again?"

"Rebecca," another person who used my full name when I hit a nerve, "you know I gave up my job to take care of the house while Kyle works. And we're trying to start a family."

"Right, marriage, the oldest profession in the book."

It did not take much for Jen to storm out on me. She made for the door but not before delivering one final blow. "Maybe you should stop feeling sorry for yourself and get on with your life. You're going to be thirty-four next month."

"A lot you know about my life. You're a part-time friend, remember?"

"I'm sorry I have other responsibilities. You should try it sometime."

Jen's words stung. Since my mother's death, I took care of my father during his struggles with diabetes. Doctors and hospitals, insulin and IV's. The hospital was my second home.

To and from, back and forth, day and night. But I never had responsibilities?

Pursued by anger, I lifted my finger to Jen's face. "You go to hell."

"Whatever!" Jen howled. She slammed the door on her way out.

Good riddance.

She was here, then gone. I was a kid, then an adult. It all happened too fast. With my mother's ring carried away by soiled water, a wave of remorse swept over me as I brushed my teeth that evening.

I discharged a mouthful of toothpaste at the mirror. "Failure," echoed from my throat. Holding a bottle of mouthwash, my left hand swung at the medicine cabinet, producing a crack in the glass. Glittery bits of debris shimmered on the bottom of the sink.

Through the bathroom window, I saw a family of four going down the street. Jealous of their smiles, the ones they wore as they walked side by side, I imagined that they were on their way to a family get-together. I knew gatherings like that back in Brooklyn.

But that was yesterday.

A photo album sat on the edge of the bookshelf in my room. When I picked it up, a snapshot of me and my mother toppled out. She was sitting in a chair looking down at me as I clung to her leg. I chucked the photo across the room like a Frisbee, unable to look at that wretched child any longer.

There was another shot of my father, his narrow body braced in a chair with me beside him. I could tell John snapped the picture by the snarl on Dad's face. The image was taken a month before he went into the hospital for the last time.

It was during that last hospital stay when my father dropped a bomb on me.

"Becky," he said, "you know I want to be cremated when I die? Promise me you'll go back to Brooklyn to spread my ashes over Mommy's grave."

"You know, Dad, when you get released we should go hiking."

My father pulled at the oxygen tubes in his nose. "Those days are gone, Becky."

"I was watching a home movie the other night. Remember how I would follow you while you filmed? God, you're a fast walker, Dad."

"Becky, I'm not the same person in the video. And I'm not going to get better this time."

My father's appearance confirmed his impending death, something he kept trying to tell me. His words died on impact. I waded through yesterday like someone unwilling to emerge from an ocean during high tide.

My father wishes, the ones I'd been putting off since his death, had to be kept. With much consternation, phone in hand, I dialed the number to the bus company.

A hoarse voice that I mistook for a man answered. "Can you tell me what time the bus leaves for New York in the morning?"

"We have one going out at four, six-fifteen, and seven-thirty," the woman replied in a raspy tone.

Plans were set. I intended to be on the seven-thirty bus to the Port Authority, then hop the subway to Brooklyn.

After twenty-four years I was going home.

I got the blue backpack from my bedroom closet and loaded it with my journal and a few books. Next, I laid out my clothes: a pair of jeans, a grey sweatshirt, and sneakers. Off the top shelf, I grabbed the small urn containing my father's remains and situated it inside my backpack.

With everything in order I climbed into bed to catch some sleep, but it would not come. I dialed John's number. Voicemail. Heather.

Halfway through Jen's number, I hung up. She'd be too busy burping Kyle or making plans with her hotsy-totsy friends, the married ones. No single chicks allowed, because they're contagious.

Music brought comfort, but the radio on my nightstand had on a local psychologist talking about life after loss. I almost broke a rib trying to turn the dial, until something caught my attention.

A woman in her fifties who'd just lost her mother was talking about how she couldn't deal with the notion of not seeing her mother again. "I can't believe Mama's gone," she said. "She was there through it all, my wedding, the birth of my children. We had breakfast together every day."

"You miss your Mama?" I mimicked. "Breakfast every morning. Give me a break! I can't even remember what my mother's food tasted like."

My relationship with my mother was frozen in childhood memories. She read me stories and we watched cartoons; she pushed me on the swings and put money under my pillow when I lost a tooth. Still, it hadn't been enough.

I'd known the mother, not the woman.

Four

The alarm sounded at 5:30. A man's voice emanated from the radio: "Good morning. It's DJ Jake with you on this glorious day of new beginnings."

A quick bowl of cereal and out the door I went with my blue backpack in tow. I walked a few blocks to an ATM and withdrew three hundred dollars. A lot of money for a day trip, but New York wasn't cheap.

I whisked through the entrance of the bus station to the ticket booth. "Thirty-eight dollars," said an employee behind the counter. My fingers stuck to the credit card as I shoved it underneath a plastic window.

Outside a light chill permeated the air, causing a shudder to run down my spine. I took my place amid the other travelers.

A large silver bus with a picture of a Greyhound turned into the station, prompting an announcement over the loud-speaker: "Now boarding at gate number 3 to New York City, Greyhound Bus 1-9-8-0."

Toward the back of the bus I noticed two empty seats. I took the one nearest the window, pleased to be sitting alone. After getting situated, I leaned back and closed my eyes.

I could hear the remaining passengers hurrying to their seats. Vibrations from the slamming of the door meant that everyone had boarded and the bus was ready to depart.

"Hello there," came a man's voice with much excitement. An instant annoyance. "Do you mind if I sit here?" He pointed to the empty seat next to me. I opened one eye, giving the bus a quick survey. All the seats were taken, and I couldn't very well ask him to sit in the restroom, though the thought had crossed my mind.

"Have a seat," I remarked with disappointment.

He was a man in his mid-seventies with a full head of short grey hair, and, despite his age, hardly any wrinkles. He wore a white polo shirt and khaki pants held up by a pair of tan suspenders. His face hardly showed signs of wear, the skin pulled tight around his eyes and mouth. He didn't give his name. I didn't bother to ask.

"Travel to New York often?" he inquired. His large hands assumed few age spots. He extracted an orange from a brown paper bag.

I grimaced before answering. "Not at all."

He began peeling the fruit, juice squirted in   every direction. "Oh, is this your first time going to the city?

It was obvious his inquiries would persist, so I gave in. "I was born in New York, Brooklyn, to be exact. That's where I'm headed."

He offered me a slice of orange, which I declined. "Are you going home for any particular reason?"

Yes, to wallow in self-pity and lose myself in a past that doesn't exist.

I bobbed my head no. There was no need to tell him the reason for my trip since I was not thrilled about what I had to do.

"Any family in Brooklyn?"

"Nope. I'm just going to look around."

The stranger propped up and looked me dead in the eyes. "Just looking for yesterday, eh?"

"What did you say?" I replied, shocked at the familiarity of his words.

A few passengers shot me a foul look, urging me, perhaps, to keep my voice down. One woman raised her brows as if I'd escaped from a mental institution.

"The past is a wonderful place to reminisce about, but when it prevents you from moving on, well, that's another problem," answered the stranger.

His audacity astounded me. I turned from his gleaming stare.

"I hope I haven't offended you?"

I twisted back around to face my antagonist. "You know nothing about me."

"Is that a fact?"

"What do you mean by that?"

"Maybe I know you better than you think." I took out a book, but he kept talking. "Let me ask you something, if you could go back to the past, would you?

Where had I heard those words before? They were my words to my grandmother, during a summer visit after she'd moved to Florida. The same question, but her answer stunned me.

"Grandma, if you were given the chance to relive your past, would you?"

"Certainly not," she replied without much thought. "I'm happy right where I am."

It was clear that she had allowed herself to become submerged in a new culture that bared no resemblance to Brooklyn. Florida's neighborhoods did not look or feel like the neighborhoods back home. Grandma had surrendered to it all, even the holidays where residents wore short-sleeved shirts instead of traditional Christmas sweaters, where hot chocolate didn't taste the same during a heatwave, and snow only fell in the snow globes Grandma brought with her from Brooklyn.

"But, Grandma, we had good times."

She tapped the fingers of her right hand off the arm of the recliner. "Becky, going back to the past wouldn't be healthy."

"Why not?"

"Because you cannot edit your life to reveal the happy moments. If you go back, you go back to everything. Even the pain."

I'd been lost in thought when I heard the stranger say, "I'm waiting?"

"Yes, if I could go back, I would."

He took the paper bag with the orange peels and opened it. "See these peels? Think of them as layers of the past."

"What are you getting at?" I scowled.

"When the peels are removed the orange isn't the same anymore. Now, you can try to put the peels back on, but you can't. That's how it is with the past. You can't put it back together, because it will never be the same."

The stranger's metaphor annoyed me, but I played his hand. "OK, what are you supposed to do then?"

"Ah," he said, pointing a finger upward. "You learn from it and let go."

"I don't have anything to learn," I responded in defiance.

"Quite the stubborn person, aren't you? Tell me the truth, why are you going to Brooklyn?"

"There's something I need to do," I replied.

"Then you're on the right path. Just make sure to stay on course."

"What do you mean?"

"It's easy to set out to do the right thing until something diverts your attention. But you must resist the urge to look back."

"I have no idea what you're talking about."

The stranger placed his hands on his lap looking like he might pray. "You will."

Two and a half hours later the Greyhound pulled into the Port Authority. My knees cracked in an attempt to stand. Youth made no difference to legs that were cramped for long periods of time. But the stranger stood without any noticeable discomfort.

I slid my arms through the straps of my backpack and waited for the other passengers to amass their belongings. Then I moved toward the door with the stranger straggling behind.

An escalator took me upstairs to an entire world inside the Port Authority: bookstores and bakeries, delis and coffee shops. I progressed through the terminal until the stranger yanked my sleeve.

"Listen, I'm sure we'll run into one another again, but I'd like you to have something." He placed his hand inside the left pocket of his slacks, and when it reemerged he handed me a subway token. "You never know when it might come in handy."

"They don't use these anymore," I interjected. "There's something called a MetroCard."

The stranger cautioned me to keep it safe.

Though he appeared out of his mind, I thanked him and deposited the token inside my backpack.

"Good luck, Rebecca," the stranger added. "Remember, don't get sidetracked." He waved as he departed and practically evaporated between a cluster of New Yorkers.

Rebecca? How did he know my name?

Along the forties, Broadway marquees were lit with titles of the latest shows. Souvenir shops lined the streets where tourists could purchase replicas of skyscrapers or anything bearing the phrase *I Love New York*.

Manhattan was crammed with people moving all around. There were cars and taxis, buses and bikes. Drivers blasted their horns as if the noise would somehow part traffic. Pedestrians strolled across busy streets undeterred of the vehicles edging toward their legs. People jammed coffee shops on the prowl for that first cup. Delis turned out delicacies at rapid speed to accommodate those in need of a quick meal.

With no time to waste in Manhattan, I set out to find the nearest subway, unmindful that one was located inside the Port Authority.

I walked half a block before stopping a woman for directions. "Can't you read?" she barked, pointing to a sign that read "SUBWAY" in bulky black letters. Who said New Yorkers weren't charming?

I saw no vending machines containing MetroCards. "Now what?" I mumbled. Over by the turnstile I noticed a coin-sized slot. Tokens were supposed to be extinct. I dug in my backpack for the one given to me by the stranger.

A mass of commuters hurried by, some plodding down on benches, others standing at attention, hidden behind *The New York Times*. Trains came and went, zigzagging and crisscrossing.

Underneath my feet I felt the tremor of the train that would take me home. Multiple subway cars whizzed by before the whole thing came to a stop. Sandwiched between heaps of people, I squeezed through the doors and procured the last available seat.

Being on the subway felt different, not at all the way it had in my youth. In those days the train was like a ride at Coney Island, the exhilaration of which no longer impressed me.

Skimming the train's interior, I noticed archaic writing. *Graffiti.* Astonished, I leaned into the person next to me and asked, "Didn't they clean up the graffiti years ago?" My question was met with a grunt, a New Yorker's cue to leave them alone.

I shifted in my seat whenever the train stopped to let passengers off and allow new ones on. I'd forgotten how the lull of the train drew people to sleep.

My eyes drooped, then closed.

Five

"Kings Highway," the conductor announced, waking me from my nap. I scrambled up a flight of stairs and went through what looked like an iron cage, where I rotated my body clockwise until being released.

I was home at last, even if it wasn't the home I'd remembered.

Sadie and I had exchanged letters after I left Brooklyn, and on numerous occasions she informed me of the changes that had taken place. She said if I ever came back I wouldn't recognize my hometown. Familiar buildings had been replaced by newer establishments.

Sadie's letters charged my mind as I crossed to the other side of Kings Highway, anxious to see the alterations but not quite ready for the transformation, because nobody had the right to tear down my memories.

The stench from overflowing garbage invaded my lungs, leaving me to pinch the tip of my nose in defense.

A homeless man laid atop a flattened piece of cardboard, his legs scrunched up against his chest. Pedestrians kept on the move, stepping over the man. One woman chided, "Get lost you bum." I scowled at the woman's ignorance, knowing that not everyone could help their circumstances. And taking a twenty dollar bill, I credited the empty tin can by his side.

As I meandered through the streets, I started to become aware of my surroundings. To my left was a young man sporting a Members Only jacket and a woman who displayed a multicolored umbrella top and a short skirt. Another lady waltzed out of a café in a navy-blue jumper with a satin top. Her shoulder pads looked like they'd been stolen from a football uniform.

Nothing appeared to coincide with the changes Sadie had written about. No renovated buildings. Clothes, hair, and makeup didn't fit the style of 2009, either. Cars were big and clunky with metal exteriors rather than plastic and long antennas instead of a shark fin.

"What's going on?" I mumbled to myself.

That's when a store sign held my attention. I looked up at the name written in black lettering against a white backdrop: CRAWHORN'S RECORDS.

It can't be.

Crawhorn's had been my father's favorite haunt, the place where he bought all his records. Sadie had written that it no longer existed. But she must have been mistaken.

Inside, rows of albums reached from one end of the store to the other. I leafed through the records with a sense of nostalgia.

I came across a Dolly Parton album my father had once owned. My parents loved Dolly and turned me into a fan by age four. My father would blast her music and stomp his feet to the rhythm, while my mother bobbed her head to Dolly's angelic voice.

"Can I help you with anything?" a short man with dark-rimmed glasses asked as I sprang to life. The Dolly album flew from my grip.

"Just looking," I answered.

The clerk glanced at the record. "Ah, one of our best sellers. We just got it in a few weeks ago."

"It's great that you still sell records," I responded, as I inserted the album back in its stack, ignorant of what the clerk had said.

He smiled, his glasses slipping to the edge of his nose. "Anytime Dolly has a new album they go fast."

New Album?

"My mom and dad loved her music. I still remember when my father brought home this record years ago."

It was like I had two heads the way the clerk stared at me.

"Well, you puzzle me when you say years ago. This record is brand new."

"Yeah, it was brand new at one time, but not in 2009."

My two heads reappeared.

"You mean 1980?"

It was obvious the man had escaped from Bellevue. "Ah, no, I mean 2009."

"Young lady, I'm not so old that I don't know what year it is."

"I know what year it is, too," I yelled while onlookers turned.

"There's no arguing with young people." The clerk waved me away before assisting other customers.

Psychopath! I couldn't be bothered with anyone's mental state. I had places to go.

The address to the cemetery rested in my hand, but I wanted to find my grandmother's old house on Crestwood Avenue first. I'd spent years declining Sadie's invitation to visit; years arguing that my father not take me to Brooklyn. Yet I found myself being seduced by the place I'd fought so long to avoid.

While under its spell I spun around to catch another oddity – The Cineplex Theater that had been torn down in the mid-nineties, according to Sadie.

They must have rebuilt it. They rebuilt it and by coincidence, they just happen to be showing The Empire Strikes Back.

Along Coney Island Avenue, a red ball bounced across the street. "Could you get my ball?" a young boy called out.

"What? Oh, yeah." I picked up the ball and bounced it off the ground as I crossed to return it.

The boy muttered something like thanks but I couldn't be sure, because I was too fixated on what he and his friends were wearing. One boy had on a yellow Dukes of Hazzard t-shirt, paired with shorts that had a double white stripe down the sides. Another kid wore blue sneakers and white tube socks stretched up his calves; around each sock was a blue and yellow stripe. A look I sported myself in the eighties.

"Why are you dressed like that?" I asked.

"Like what?" one boy replied.

"Those clothes are from the eighties."

All the kids bowed in hysterics. "No foolin!"

I backed up and went on my way, but not before turning to catch the boys flapping their arms, repeating, "Cuckoo, cuckoo."

Between E. 14th and E. 15th Street, Joe's Deli stood resurrected, as grocers strolled out with bundles in their arms. Mothers in housecoats swept front stoops with curlers dangling from their hair. Three young men wearing red bandanas and denim vests shook cans of spray paint as they eyed garage doors. A middle-aged man with an Irish brogue ran at the hoodlums with a shovel, threatening to crack their skulls in if they didn't scram.

I couldn't untangle my mind. Everything looked as it had in my youth. It left me perplexed like I'd misplaced my marbles. Yet at the same time I embraced the intimate ambiance of home.

When my shoelace came untied I stopped to fasten it and noticed a sign above my head that read McNally Park. I'd spent my early childhood playing on the swings and coasting down the metal sliding board. The park had been updated to include modern swings, a plastic slide, a teeter-totter, and a sandbox. But as I looked around I saw two things: swings and a metal sliding board.

Mystified, I walked through the park while the sun's intensity scorched the top of my head; my vision impaired by black and white static. The sweatshirt I wore wreaked of perspiration; wet circles stained each armpit.

In a small crowd, a memorable face appeared. A woman. There was a child at her side. I cupped my hands around my eyes to ward off the glimmer of the sun.

It can't be.

I gathered my arms around my abdomen; fierce pain escalated inside. Breathlessness. A sudden chill traveled my body. I inspected the woman's face a second time.

Sadie.

And the child beside her with short brown hair and light blue eyes, wearing a blue and white Smurf shirt and black shorts, she was someone I knew, too, because she was me!

Both knees buckled, sending me face first onto the torrid concrete.

Six

My heart should have been jubilant seeing Sadie peering over me. But one problem persisted: Sadie was dead.

A young man playing handball ran over to where I lay and elevated me to my feet. "Are you alright?" he asked.

How could I tell? It wasn't often deceased people came to life, so I was ill-prepared to handle such a situation.

"Do you need a glass of wuta?" Sadie inquired in her thick Brooklyn accent where the letter R had no relevance.

Photographs that had accompanied Sadie's letters depicted an older version of my former babysitter. This Sadie, however, still had brown hair sprinkled with salt and pepper. Her face revealed minimal wrinkles. She seemed alert, the Alzheimer's nowhere in sight. This was the Sadie I remembered from childhood.

"You seem a little confused," Sadie remarked. "It must be the heat."

That and the fact that my dead babysitter is holding my hand as a child.

I couldn't look at Sadie hard enough, long enough; my heart gushed with elation. And it wasn't just the presence of an old friend that caused delight, but the notion that for whatever reason, I had been carried back to my past.

The world offered no explanations. Had the past always existed like a dark shadow in some other realm?

"What's your name?" Sadie asked. She didn't recognize me. How could she?

I decided to use my middle name so I wouldn't be confused with the child. "Lynn."

"What a nice name. I'm Sadie."

Indeed.

"And the little one is Rebecca. Say hello, Becky." The child turned away and burrowed her face in Sadie's back.

"Do you live around here? I've never seen you before," Sadie said while I looked at the child hiding behind her.

"No, I'm from Pennsylvania."

"Oh, oh. Are you visiting family?"

If Sadie was alive, maybe they all were: my grandmother and aunts, my father and my . . . mother.

"No, my family isn't from here," I lied hesitantly.

"You still look a little shaken. Why don't you come home with me and have some lunch?"

It wasn't unlike Sadie to invite someone she'd just met to her home. She made friends with everyone who crisscrossed the borough of Brooklyn.

I ignored the consistent whisper urging me to go straight to the cemetery and told Sadie I'd be delighted.

Sadie held the child's hand as we walked through the iron gates of McNally Park headed for Crestwood Avenue, where not only Sadie lived, but my family.

Rows of houses stood alongside one another with not much space in between. Backyards could fit a picnic table and a small garden, but nothing more. The surrounding buildings had fire escapes with horizontal platforms that connected to stairs. They provided Brooklynites with a place to hang out during hot summers, while teenagers used them as an escape when their parents were asleep.

I'd spent the better part of my childhood in a place where neighbors knew one another on a first name basis; when block parties and barbeques occupied most summer evenings; when you could walk through the neighborhood and be greeted by recognizable faces.

Although I hadn't laid eyes on Crestwood in twenty-four years, the memories were never far from my mind. I trailed behind Sadie and the child while my hometown reeled me in.

We had just turned the corner when something beckoned my attention. The stranger.

He looked about ten feet high from where I was standing. My heart palpitated, as I gestured for him to be gone. He didn't heed my warning, nor did I heed his. The stranger didn't speak; he didn't have to. I could read his face alerting me to turn back.

Seven

Sadie looked around to see who I was responding to, but there was no one that she could see.

Adrenaline hastened my footsteps as the ground beneath moved steadily. I raced to Sadie's front gate. The breath had been knocked from my lungs, so I knelt to salvage whatever air was left.

Over my shoulder I could see Sadie dragging her bad leg to catch up, the child lagging in the background. The stranger had gone; something told me it wouldn't be for long.

I could tell by the disconcerted look on Sadie's face that my actions confused her. I didn't try to explain, hoping she would dismiss the incident. She had a better question in mind: "How did you know which house was mine?"

I moved away from the child who was whacking the fence with a stick she'd recovered from the ground. I turned back to Sadie whose demand for an answer became prominent by her facial expression.

"Lucky guess, no?"

Sadie squinted through her glasses, trying to discern the situation before sauntering through the gate and up the porch steps.

A small brick building rested in the background, which had once appeared enormous, but had lost its colossal stature.

Two large windows with white trim took over the front of the building, and a window shaped liked a diamond relaxed in the middle of the door.

I stood at the base of the steps feeling my way through the memories; pawing the banister I used to slide down.

Sadie paused before opening the door. Then came the burning question, the one she was unable to sustain. "Why did you run a little while ago?"

I stumbled to provide an answer, knowing that if the truth were known, I'd be hauled off to Bellevue by men in white coats. I took a tissue from my back pocket and patted the tiny grains of sweat dribbling down my face.

"I saw something." What that something was I could not admit. But Sadie, she figured it out. Or so she thought.

"Was it the dog on the corner? He won't bother you. Mrs. Whitendale has him for protection ever since her husband ran off with that stewardess. You know, she's nervous about all the crime we've been having. She depended on Carl, her husband, for protection. Poor thing is afraid of her own shadow. She jumps when a car backfires. Last Fourth of July the kids down the street lit firecrackers, and Mrs. Whitendale just about dropped dead.

Carl, he's a pilot for a major airline, and he was having an affair with one of his stewardesses. I was on my porch talking to Meg, that's the neighbor down the block, when Mrs. Whitendale, Clara is her name, chased Carl, that's her husband, down the stoop with a baseball bat, hollering for him to get out and go be with his," Sadie put her hands over the child's ears, "*trollop*." Oh, yea, it was a big brouhaha."

Good old Sadie. She had a childlike innocence that made her loveable. While I worried that she would question my sanity for running from an invisible man, she filled me in on the latest neighborhood gossip in classic Sadie style.

The stranger's words came fluttering back. "Stay on course," he'd advised. I was in Brooklyn to scatter my father's ashes, but my plans were altered once the past welcomed me home. Nothing would stop me from reuniting with the mother who had forsaken me.

Everything in the eighties was plastered in the same dull colors: green, yellow, orange, and brown. Sadie's petite kitchen was no exception. A dark green wall oven on the far left matched the refrigerator sitting in the corner. The counter space was minimal but held a small toaster and two orange canisters. A half-wall separated the kitchen from the dining room, where I saw an oval table underneath a plastic tablecloth. On the wall hung an avocado rotary telephone with an over-stretched cord that touched the floor. There was a hall leading to the bathroom; beyond that, three bedrooms.

The child dove off a red armchair onto a black ottoman, which she turned on its side and used to roll on her stomach. The gold colored couch also bore plastic - a good idea to keep furniture clean, unless the plastic cracked and you sat down. And God forbid you had shorts on.

Sadie hobbled over to the television and turned it on so the child could watch her favorite program, *The Magic Garden*, a children's show where two adult women in pigtails - one with a guitar – swayed back and forth on swings that fell from the sky, while singing catchy tunes and playing with objects inside a large trunk.

"Would you like a bologna sangwich?" Sadie asked.

"Yes, thank you," I answered cordially.

I sat at the table while Sadie made lunch. The child grew bored with the ottoman and followed Sadie into the kitchen. She amused herself by opening and closing cabinets.

"I haven't forgotten your potato chips," Sadie remarked.

She placed the food and drinks on the table, then let out a sigh. "Sometimes this leg is impossible."

The chips where nearest my end, but the child snatched the tall cylinder away from my reach.

"Ohhhh, Becky, that isn't nice," Sadie scolded. "Axe before you take things."

I snickered as Sadie spoke Brooklynese.

"What's funny?" Sadie wondered.

"Your accent. I haven't heard it in a while." The words slipped from my mouth and hovered in the air, putting my identity and sanity in jeopardy.

"When did you ever hear my accent?" Sadie asked.

I wasn't good at making excuses on short notice, but Sadie looked on in anticipation.

"I've heard the Brooklyn accent in movies."

Sadie bought it, but the child giggled. I shook my head, displeased by her mere presence.

When she finished her sandwich, the child left the table and pulled out a yellow lunchbox. She opened the lid and dumped small figures onto the floor. I rose from my chair for a better view.

"Dolly Pops!" I said. The child disregarded my comment and resumed her play. She took a plastic doll and snapped a dress on it.

I picked one up, but the child smacked it from my hand.

"Now, Becky," Sadie reproached, "share your toys." She spoke as if it were perfectly normal for adults to play with tiny plastic dolls. And maybe in Sadie's world, it was.

The child inspected me as I stared back at her. She was just a kid, but I wondered if her instincts revealed my identity. I couldn't be certain. Still, I didn't appreciate her defiant sneer as she popped dresses on and off her dolls.

"Tell me all about yourself," remarked Sadie still seated at the table.

"You want to know about my life?"

"Yea, yea!" Sadie grinned as bits of chips fell from her mouth.

During a commercial the child went to the TV and started chanting a familiar, yet annoying, phrase I hadn't heard in years. "PIX, PIX, PIX."

"There's nothing much to tell," I grumbled, turning from the television. My life is rather boring." I deflected from the conversation and took my plate into the kitchen. The phone rang and Sadie asked me to answer it.

"Hello?"

"Is Sadie there? This is Meg."

"Just a minute," I said handing Sadie the phone while keeping steady the cord that pivoted every which way. The child continued to yell out, "PIX, PIX, PIX."

"Hello, Meg. Yea, yea, I'm babysitting. Stop over for cawfee. There's someone I want you to meet. Awlright. Sooo long."

My heart warmed as Sadie hung up the phone. It was nice to see friendship the way it was meant to be. Meg and Sadie spoke regularly by phone and made time for coffee; both were married, even though Meg was a widow. I wasn't wrong after all, friends made time for one another.

After helping Sadie with the dishes there was a knock at the door. "I bet that's Meg. Would you get the door, Lynn?" Sadie asked. "Now look through the peephole. It might be a burglar."

Thieves waited until dark to make their move. But in Brooklyn anything was possible. Knock, knock. Who's there? A burglar.

"Hi! Is Sadie home?" Meg, dear Meg. I remembered her cat-eye glasses and hair like fresh snow. She was short and broad, her thunderous voice boomed down the hallway.

"Hiya, Meg." Sadie said, shuffling a deck of cards.

"Well, how are you today, Sadie?"

"I can't complain, Meg." The child seized the cards as they lay across the shiny plastic tablecloth.

"Oh, oh, Becky. That isn't nice. You should axe when you want something."

I snickered again at Sadie's unique pronunciation.

"Sadie, aren't you going to introduce me to your new friend?" Meg said.

"Yea, yea. We met this morning at the park. Meg, this is Lynn."

"Sadie always manages to make new friends."

"One minute I was pushing Becky on the swings and the next thing I know there's a woman passed out on the ground. I say it's this heat."

Meg shook her head. "That's our Sadie, everyone's mother and grandmother."

"There's something so familiar about her, don't you agree, Meg?"

The can of cola I was holding dropped from my hand and the liquid scampered across the plastic tablecloth with my napkin chasing after it.

Yes, Sadie. Remember. Please try.

"She reminds me of my cousin from Long Island."

Blasted.

"I don't doubt your word, Sadie." Then turning her attention to me, Meg asked, "Are you from around here."

"She's from Pennsylvania," Sadie interjected.

"Very nice! What brings you to Brooklyn?" Meg queried.

I caressed the bottom of my backpack hanging on the chair. The past and present got in the ring. The gloves were on. Sadie's smiling face declared a winner.

"I'm looking to find an apartment around here."

"The upstairs apartment at my house is vacant if you'd like to see it," Meg said. "My son and daughter-in-law just moved out. It's furnished, too."

"That would be wonderful," I said with excitement. But as always, Sadie didn't miss a trick.

"Don't you have any belongings besides a knapsack?"

"I sort of left in a hurry."

"Oh, oh. You ain't in any trouble, are you?"

Only if the stranger catches me.

"No trouble. Just looking for a second chance, that's all."

Meg did me a favor by agreeing that two hundred and eighty dollars would be enough for the first month's rent, all the money I had left after giving twenty dollars to the homeless man. I would need a job and quick.

Sprawled across the sofa the child snored over the opening credits of *The Guiding Light*.

The clock was ticking, each minute dwindling into the next; my family would be home by six.

"So, the child's, I mean, Becky's parents live around here?" I asked, pretending not to already know.

"Three houses down," Sadie answered, directing her finger to the left side of the window. "Becky's grandma will be here later to pick her up."

"Must be crowded with everyone under one roof?" came my unintentional response.

My parents lived with my grandmother and her brother Albert. Aunt Elizabeth and Aunt Bernice lived in the downstairs apartment. I wasn't supposed to know that. But I did.

Fascinated by my exceptional awareness, Sadie exclaimed, "You sure have good instincts."

The child was still fast asleep, one hand underneath a cushion, the other lifeless, as it dangled over the edge of the sofa. Her short, fine hair looked like it'd been caught in a windstorm.

With only a few hours to go until my mother and I saw one another again, my questions were careless and uncontrolled. "I can't wait to see Ann!"

"How'd you know Ann's name?" Sadie asked.

"My, you know many things," Meg replied as she pulled at the shirt riding up her curvy figure.

"Yeah, yeah," Sadie added. "I think she's . . ., oh, what's the name for those people with instincts?"

"Psychic," Meg declared.

Something roused the child into an upright position. She looked distraught. Sadie reached over to pat her back. "What's wrong, Becky?"

The child looked at Sadie and rubbed her eyes, tiny spots of water swayed from her lashes.

I strived to answer how I knew my mother's name. "You mentioned Ann's name earlier, don't you remember?" How I hated to make Sadie feel like her memory was going so soon.

Scratching her head she responded, "I don't remember that. But if you say so."

Then Sadie recruited Meg to help retrieve something from the bedroom closet. The child sat on the floor, fully engrossed in a conversation with herself.

"I wish some people would go away."

"Who are you talking to?" I asked.

"My friend."

"I don't see anyone."

"He said you can't be here."

"Who said?"

"I told you, my friend."

"Don't mind her," Sadie said, limping to the couch. "She always talks to her imaginary friend."

I wanted to press the issue further, but Meg was anxious to show me my new apartment. She waltzed me out the door with Sadie shadowing.

The desire to see my mother was intense. I needed a reason to see her, and Sadie could make it happen.

"Would it be OK if I come by a little later, Sadie?"

"Ohhh, of course. You can have dinner with me. My husband is working late tonight. I could use the company."

The deal was set. Sadie would introduce me to my grandmother when she came to pick up the child; in turn, my grandmother would bring me to my mother.

Meg relayed stories about every neighbor along Crestwood Avenue. I recognized the homes but not the stories about their occupants.

"Over there," Meg stated, "that's where Trish and Ed live. They're alright, but Trish drinks. She's a harmless pain in the neck. Always pestering everyone for loose change, you know what I mean? And the family across from Trish and Ed, stay clear of them altogether. Mitchell, the son, he's a little off the wall." Meg brought her finger up to her temple and made a circular motion. "He and his sister live with their elderly mother. Poor old woman. They take every pension and social security check from her. Last week Mitchell was in his boxer shorts hollering at a stop sign, some gibberish like 'how dare you leave me like that.' What a spectacle."

Meg's accounts flabbergasted me. I knew these people, or thought I did. Trish and Ed took walks in the evening, amiable and always shaking everyone's hand. Mitchell, well, I didn't remember much about him, though the story about the stop sign sounded like something I'd heard before.

As Meg prattled on about the neighbors, she realized I was immobile. "Is everything OK?"

It wasn't the remodeled home I'd heard about in Sadie's letters. The white picket fence was still attached to the green trellis. The front yard was lush with fruit trees – cherry and apple. Elevated above the garage on the left-hand side, a small open patio where Aunt Elizabeth and Aunt Bernice spent weekends reading the paper when the weather permitted. Around the other end of the house, a porch leading to the main entrance.

Meg could hardly comprehend my fascination, but she waited as I imbibed the spirit of my grandmother's house and the tranquility that accompanied it.

"This is where Becky's family lives," Meg said, breaking the silence. "You'll meet them later on."

The mere suggestion of reuniting with my kin was electrifying, yet it petrified me all the same. How would I react when the lost souls of my family, restored by some unexplained breath of life, found their way into my world?

Or had I found my way into theirs? It was hard to tell.

Meg and I continued toward her house. Unbeknownst to my tour guide, my mind was cluttered with thoughts of my mother.

What would our relationship be like after her long absence? She'd been gone so long that memories felt more like hallucinations. Even photographs revealed a woman who'd become unfamiliar, someone I knew, but could hardly remember how.

Meg led me inside the home she once shared with her husband. Though the outside of the house looked up to date, the interior remained locked in a time capsule.

The damp, musty odor smacked my face as I entered. Meg's furniture looked like it was borrowed from an episode of *Father Knows Best*. Even the telephone hadn't been updated. It was one of those heavy black phones, the kind that made your arm fall asleep if you held the receiver too long. The console radio sitting in the corner by the sofa still worked, and Meg wasted no time turning it on. While music filled her nostalgic home, I promenaded through each room evaluating Meg's distinct taste for antiquity.

"Let's go upstairs so you can see where you'll be staying," Meg exclaimed.

If Meg's dwelling was reminiscent of the fifties, the upstairs apartment captured the core of the eighties. Dark paneling comprised most of the walls. Floral wallpaper with soft pastels covered the kitchen. A wooden table with orange cushioned chairs lay in the middle of the kitchen floor with an overview of track lighting. A small Zenith TV with rabbit ears sat on a stand near two bookcases in the living room.

I hope you like it, Meg said.

Hideous!

The beige AT&T telephone on the end table started to ring. "Hello? Sadie, yes, she loves the place, especially the decorations. You had to see her face when she saw them. I'll send her over in a few minutes." She put the phone back down. "Sadie said dinner is almost ready," Then Meg reached into her pocketbook and handed me a key to the front door.

I took my sweaty palms and skated them down the sides of my jeans. The rug beneath my feet showed signs of wear, my manic state didn't help as I paced back and forth. Meg got in the middle of my march to observe the red welts sprouting on my neck. She was talking to me. I could hear a deafening echo coming from her mouth as she called out my name.

Fade in. Fade out.

Sadie was on the porch as I fidgeted with the latch on her gate. I never could get it open. Nothing had changed.

As I took to the stairs an unmistakable voice rang out.

"Hi, Sadie."

I closed my eyes tight. My grandmother came around the corner.

"Hi, Flo. How was work today?" Sadie asked.

"Same as always. Crazy."

The child flew down the steps past Sadie, pushed me out of the way, and jumped into my grandmother's arms.

"I made this for you, Gramma," she said holding up a page from her Bugs Bunny Coloring Book.

"Very nice, Becky. You kept in the lines, too."

"She was a good girl today, weren't you, Becky?" Sadie said as she held onto the white banister.

Though I'd last seen my grandmother in her eighties, she resurfaced with medium length blond hair instead of the short white cut she sported later on. She had on black slacks and a navy-blue blouse covered by a white sweater. Her firm hands clutched the strap of her pocketbook.

"Flo, I want you to meet our new neighbor. I met her today at McNally Park."

Sadie explained the story while my knees wobbled like the legs on a broken table. Just as the introductions ended, Grandma extended her hand. "Nice to meet you."

I stiffened like a mannequin and whispered hello. My grandmother received me like a visitor, cordial but lacking the attachment we had shared the first time around. Just like with Sadie, I meant nothing to my grandmother; an outsider in a strange land that nobody knew.

"Well, I'd better be running along and get dinner started. The gang will be home soon."

"That's right," Sadie answered. "Flo, where's Albert today?"

"Where do you think? At the bar with his filthy friends."

Albert was my grandmother's younger brother. He lived with Grandma because he didn't have enough income to live on his own.

"Stop by around seven-thirty for coffee and dessert, Sadie."

"You don't have to axe me twice."

My fingers crossed behind my back.

"You, too, Lynn."

Bingo.

The deal was set, paralyzed though it left me. Although having my parents restored to good health brought joy, the idea of meeting my mother as an adult put pressure on my heart. I hadn't intended to collide with my past. There were no instructions on how to maneuver through this fantastical world.

But one thing was clear - letting go was no longer an option. I would not return to the present if it meant sending my family back to their graves.

Eight

Sadie's leftover meatloaf lodged in my throat. Twice she got up to smack my back. "You remind me of Becky. You both eat too fast."

While Sadie did the dishes, I thumbed through a copy of TV Guide, a staple inside every household in the eighties. I lit up upon seeing the titles of my favorite shows: *The Facts of Life, The Dukes of Hazzard, Three's Company, Different Strokes, Little House on the Prairie, The Incredible Hulk.* I knew no titles of shows in 2009. Most of them were reality-based. I preferred fantasy.

By seven-twenty we left for my grandmother's, as Sadie dazzled me with more stories I didn't know about the neighbors.

Upon approaching the white picket fence my heart flinched with dread. While the impending reunion with my mother gratified me, it remained uncertain whether I could bear the encounter. She wouldn't recognize me in my adult body. For twenty-four long years, I had ached for the child to disappear and the adult to take her place.

"I can't. I can't go in there, Sadie." I gripped the fence with both hands and held on.

"What's the matter? Are you ill?"

"Just a little nervous."

"Oh, oh. Well, you mustn't be nervous. They're very nice people. Before you know it, you'll be just like family."

Sadie took me by the hand as we crossed from the trellis to the brick staircase. She rang the bell and through the tinted glass, an outline of a woman emerged.

Aunt Elizabeth.

"Come on in, come on in," she said.

Aunt Elizabeth, my grandmother's older sister, had been my rock during the turbulent times in my life. I had leaned on her for advice, though scarcely taking any of it. She had an immaculate complexion and auburn hair and fingernails painted red. Her small figure belied her fierce personality.

"Hi there, Elizabeth," Sadie said. "How are you?"

"Not too shabby," Aunt Elizabeth retorted.

Upon hearing the chatter, Aunt Bernice stopped by the door and flashed her infectious smile.

Aunt Bernice was Grandma's and Aunt Elizabeth's cousin. My aunts shared living expenses and remained single, much to the consternation of those who regarded single women as an atrocity.

"Hello, Sadie." Bernice's amiable temperament made her favorable among family and friends. In her stocking feet, she towered over most people. Her dark, flat hair had begun to discolor. Red reading glasses slithered down her nose.

"Girls, I want you to meet Lynn. I met her at the park today."

My Aunts greeted me in their genial manner with hugs rather than handshakes. "I hope you enjoy Brooklyn," Aunt Bernice exclaimed.

Aunt Elizabeth aimed her perfectly lined teeth at me. "It'll take some getting used to living around here. I hope you can handle it."

Within a few years my aunts, unable to keep up with the high cost of living, would retire to Florida until their deaths. Though I visited them every summer, I missed these aunts, the ones who went to Broadway shows and dinner parties, who drove new cars instead of used. Their souls had been repaired to match bodies that had not yet frayed.

Sadie and I mounted the stairs to Grandma's apartment where the aroma of freshly brewed coffee drifted through the cracks of the door.

"Will we be seeing you two later?" Sadie called down to my aunts.

"A little later. I'm working on a crossword puzzle," answered Aunt Elizabeth.

Sadie produced a fist and knocked on the alabaster door. I needed something to grip, so I took a pile of her coat. I tucked in my lower lip to hide the quiver.

"Why are you squirming?" Sadie didn't know that beyond the door lived my family, all of whom, like Sadie, were supposed to be dead and buried.

I should have left. The stranger wanted me to. And for that very reason, I didn't. Twenty-four years of being a motherless daughter kept me in place.

Grandma answered the door wearing a green smock and white slippers. She had a limp dishrag slung over her right shoulder. "Well, you made it."

I staggered onto the vinyl carpet protector and wiped my shoes. "Sadie," Grandma said, "show our guest around." But I knew every step. The home devoured me and put to rest the reclusive world I'd left behind. I moved with ease, inspecting each room with diligence.

The breakfront adjacent to the doorway housed china that had belonged to my great-grandmother. There was a dining table to the right beneath a crystal chandelier, and a varnished credenza in the far corner. Just how I'd remembered.

Behind the blue couch, a picture window concealed by thick blinds and white curtains containing a flowery pattern that ran along the base; parallel to the couch, a love seat leaned against the wall with a mirror suspended above. Uncle Albert's favorite chair bore holes from overuse. Around the corner, his bedroom. The upstairs contained additional bedrooms.

I heard movement in the kitchen and when I went to investigate, I found a tall figure leaning against the sink. He was dressed in a white t-shirt, dungarees, and black loafers. Beneath his russet hair, his face disclosed a pallid complexion.

Dad.

He was sipping coffee and munching cookies, oblivious to the fact that in a few years his life would be complicated by sugar.

"Frank," Grandma said, "this is Lynn. She comes from Pennsylvania."

Dad shook his head and waved his cookie in the air. He had no way of foreseeing the hellish years ahead when his body would betray and imprison him.

"Don't mind him," declared Grandma. "He's a little shy with new people."

I tried not to think about the embers placed in the urn. He, like my mother, needed to be saved. How I was going to stop illness from ransacking my parents' bodies, I had not a clue. But something had to be done.

Uncle Albert stumbled out of his room and turned on the television to watch his favorite program, horseracing. Besides his incessant taste for the drink, he had a special fondness for ponies.

In my youth, I failed to realize that gambling plagued my great-uncle. Rather, I saw a man who enjoyed animals. His sudden outbursts of "Come on you horse's ass," had never fazed me, even when Grandma shouted at him to put away the racing form and get a real job.

"Turn that television off for God's sake. We have company. And wash that greasy hair, will you?" Grandma laid into Uncle Albert like a mother disciplining her child.

"Gaw head," Uncle Albert responded, beating his arm at the air.

I couldn't help but grin as I listened to Grandma spar with Uncle Albert. Abbott and Costello all the way.

The creaking floor broke my concentration. Tiny bumps ran along my spine. I sensed her presence. Suddenly, it all came back: birthday parties, holidays, amusement parks, silly songs, and summers at the beach. The flu, earaches, sore throats. Joy, love, humor.

Then a rush of grief. The cancer. The wake. The burial. Pain, tears, anguish, guilt, prayers for her return, and the disappointment that followed when she didn't.

Mommy!

Her dark brown hair looked jet black, and her chopped bangs were parted in the middle. She was wearing a blue sweatshirt emblazoned with a Universal Studios logo in the middle. She had on dungarees and silver moccasins.

My eyes steadied on her without blinking, for I feared that closing them even for a second would send her back into the unknown.

"Hi, I'm Ann. You must be Lynn?" Her resonant voice commanded my attention.

She was there in the flesh, and I could touch her and she could touch me. Tears started down my cheeks and around my chin. She had no idea why either, but, for whatever reason, she let me have the moment.

"It's very nice to meet you," I answered, taking her hand. I wanted her to know who I was, who she was, and what the desolate years without her had done to me.

She knew the child, not the woman.

Mom moved in for a closer look. "I'm sorry if I stare. There is something familiar about you."

Yes! Please, Mommy, remember.

Sadie began to laugh. "I thought the same thing, Ann. Doesn't she look like my cousin Renee from Long Island? You met Renee last time she came for a visit, remember?"

"Yes, that must be it." My mother didn't seem convinced but accepted Sadie's response nonetheless.

My left leg twisted around my right, then the reverse. I bolted my hands together to prevent any visible tremor.

Grandma brought in cake and coffee. The child came galloping down the stairs, sliding across the brown carpet in a pair of Bert and Ernie slippers. A box dropped out of her hands onto the floor, spilling its contents. "She loves Colorforms," Grandma said, shaking her head at the adhesive vinyl shapes scattered about.

Dad wandered in from the kitchen and sat at the head of the table nearest the wall. He poured what had to be his third cup of coffee, adding cream and two sugars, then sliced into the cake. His sweet tooth made me cringe. I wasn't a doctor, but I feared that my father's favorite pastime would lead to insulin three times a day.

"You know," I began, "too much sugar isn't good for you."

It was out of place to add my two bits, and the reaction given by my family supported as much. I wanted my father to understand my need to interfere, but he didn't. He couldn't, because he didn't know what I knew.

"He's OK," my mother said. "This is just part of our Italian heritage." Everyone laughed, except me.

"Coffee?" Grandma asked as I thought about cautioning Dad a second time to release the cake and save himself.

"No, thank you. I don't drink coffee. I'm more of a tea person."

"Something you and my daughter have in common. I'll get a tea bag."

When my tea was ready, I washed down a slice of coffee cake and listened as everyone conversed about the hottest topic of 1980 – who shot J.R.

"How about his brother?" Sadie inquired.

My mother put down her tea. "No, I don't think it was Bobby. He's too good to do something like that. Maybe Sue Ellen. She's been drinking again."

"Why would Sue Ellen want to shoot J.R.?" Grandma asked.

"Are you kidding? She's a drunk, Ma, and he's been a thorn in her side since the beginning of the season." Mom lifted the cup to her mouth and took a sip of tea, then another.

"So what!" Uncle Albert yelled from his favorite chair. "I have a few beers now and then, but that doesn't make me a killer."

"Keep quiet!" Grandma answered. "Nobody's talking to you. And turn that damn television off."

In the middle of the debate, the aunts came up from downstairs. "Who do you think shot J.R.?" Sadie asked, filling her cup with Sanka.

Aunt Elizabeth could solve the toughest cliffhanger, but this saga stumped even her. I delighted in spilling the beans.

"It was Kristin."

The family looked on as if I'd just given inside information on Amelia Earhart's whereabouts.

My father continued adding sugar to his body. My mother took two more slurps of tea while Grandma and the ladies contemplated the possibility of Kristin being the lone shooter.

"That could be," Aunt Elizabeth said. "What made you think of her?"

"She's his mistress. He's a dog. It happens." The family would have to wait until the fall to learn that I was correct.

The dialogue shifted to a more personal nature.

Sadie was head conspirator. "We still don't know much about you. Not that we want to pry."

All eyes found their way to me. Would divulging elements of my life – our lives - set off alarm bells? Anything I told them would be used to rebuild future events. What would be the harm in that?

Still, I had to be delicate about such things.

"Any siblings?" Mom asked.

Many times my mother wished for more children, but it wasn't to be. "I'm an only child."

"Oh, that's too bad." Grandma grabbed the coffee pot and poured another cup.

Sadie tapped her head like she was trying to unleash a burning question. "What about your parents?"

I looked over at my mother who sat on the edge of her seat, and my father who was shoveling more cake into his mouth, wishing they could somehow take refuge against the destiny that awaited them.

"I'm not comfortable talking about my parents," I answered. The family did their best to disguise their disappointment.

The conversation dropped and my parents lingered in ignorance. Given time, I would find a way to save them.

When my mother got up to salvage what was left of the coffee cake, a sparkle shone from her right hand. The initial ring. Funny how I hadn't noticed it earlier.

"I love your ring, M…, Ann." How I longed to call her Mom.

She beamed with pride. "Thank you. It was a gift from the girls at work for my birthday."

The girls at work?

"Oh, I thought perhaps Frank gave it to you."

Mom laughed. "Frank would never shop for jewelry. He didn't even pick out my wedding band, my mother did."

The lost ring that resided in a dusky sewer somewhere in the present had not been from my father after all. Did it even matter?

As the evening wore on the family disbanded. Uncle Albert retreated to his room with a bottle of beer; Aunt Elizabeth and Aunt Bernice to their apartment. Dad stayed with the dessert, shaking his leg underneath the table while coffee danced around his cup.

Grandma and my mother walked Sadie and me to the door. "When are you having that Tupperware Party?" Sadie asked my mother. Inside every home on Crestwood were orange canisters, brown pitchers, white salt and pepper shakers, and multi-colored bowls.

"This Sunday," Mom answered. The child came over to where we were standing.

"Can I come, too, Mommy?" she implored through her nose.

"Becky," my grandmother interrupted, "you don't have to go everywhere with Mommy. She's not running away."

The child hugged my mother's inner thigh unable to fathom being separated, even momentarily.

"Maybe Daddy can take you to a movie. *The Empire Strikes Back* is playing at the Cineplex."

"Stay with me, Mommy, please!" The child flung herself on the floor and stamped her feet.

"Rebecca!" My mother took the child's arm and raised her from the floor, a perplexing look etched across her face. "There will be plenty of time for Tupperware Parties when you're older."

Of course the child knew better. She detected loss better than most. It was her gift. Or, perhaps, her curse.

"See you soon," I told my mother as I walked out the door. She nodded despite my need for more reassurance. Sadie strode down the block to her house leaving me in the opposite direction to Meg's.

Darkness ascended in every direction save for the streetlights which cast a warm glow around my feet.

Tingling on the base of my neck warned of something amiss. I rotated my head to the right just as the stranger surfaced.

"Rebecca, don't go on with this," he pleaded.

My feet continued in stride as I climbed the stairs to Meg's and rooted through my pocket for the key, cautious that the stranger was still on my trail.

The door opened and Meg appeared in a flannel nightgown covered by a burgundy robe. And the stranger, he was gone. But he would return. That much I knew.

"I'm sorry, Meg," I said. "I didn't mean to disturb you."

"Nonsense," she shot back. "I was up listening to the radio and having a cup of tea. Care to join me?"

"I'm rather tired. I think I'll go upstairs to bed." Meg locked up and slipped back into her apartment. I had no idea it would be the last time I'd see her.

Nine

Nineteen Eighty-One.

My body swam in the magnificence of morning while the sun gleamed through the window. I stretched as far as my arms would reach, then wiped the night's residue from the corners of my mouth. Propelling myself upward, I looked around the room, which to my astonishment, wasn't the bedroom I had fallen asleep in the night before.

"Where am I?"

The clothes I'd fallen asleep in were gone. In their place, a pair of red cotton pajamas. I ran to the hall so that I could go downstairs to find Meg, but it wasn't there. I was no longer on the second floor of Meg's house either. It was the first floor of an apartment building.

I opened the front door and stood outside in my pajamas. The door next to mine had a doorbell. I pressed my finger against the button and heard an outbreak of chimes.

"Oh, Lynn, it's you. Everything OK?"

A woman in a housecoat and curlers peered in my direction. She knew my name.

"Who are you?"

A rapid fit of laughter overcame the tiny woman. "I'm your landlady, Mrs. Russo. My, but you are groggy this morning."

Her square face and projected jaw sparked some recognition. She owned an apartment building on Avenue T.

"Where's Meg?" I sang out like I'd just awakened from a coma.

"Meg from around the corner? She passed away in January. You were at her funeral, don't you remember?"

But I didn't remember. Not an inkling of anything that had taken place except meeting Sadie and Meg and my family, having tea and cake, dodging questions about my personal life, Uncle Albert and his beer, running from the stranger, and falling asleep the night before.

"Meg's dead? How can that be?"

Then I remembered that Meg died in January of 1981. Hers was the first funeral I attended as a kid. I wandered into the funeral parlor squeezing my mother's hand. And there was Meg, laid out in a bronze casket, her son and daughter-in-law in a receiving line, greeting mourners. I hid behind my mother, because although Meg was dead, I swore her chest was heaving in and out. But my mother told me it was an illusion because I was used to seeing Meg alive.

"Are you sure you're OK?" Mrs. Russo asked.

I wasn't sure about anything. It was a mystery how I'd gotten to the past in the first place and an even bigger mystery how I'd ended up skipping a year ahead.

"What year is this?" I asked to be sure. The question resounded from my mouth and practically stupefied Mrs. Russo.

"Oh, Lynn, do you need to see a doctor? It's 1981."

"What am I doing here?"

"I rented you an apartment after Meg died."

"Who pays the rent?"

Mrs. Russo stepped back.

"You pay the rent with money you make from this thing called a job."

Job?

"I work?"

"Um, yeah, at Bargain Town. Meg got you the job after you moved to Brooklyn. She knew the owner, Mr. Ricci. He was a friend of her husband's."

Mrs. Russo continued to stare me down like my arms were bound in a white coat.

"Right, yeah, I remember," I fibbed.

"Now don't forget, Flo's barbecue is at noon."

"What barbecue?"

"It's Memorial Day, remember?" remarked Mrs. Russo. "Flo's having her annual barbecue."

Mrs. Russo left me in confusion. I went inside to make sure my backpack was still there. It was in the bedroom by the nightstand, all contents still inside.

I mused over time travel, the notion of moving forward and jumping backward. It never seemed possible, yet it had happened; more than that, it had allowed me to go from one year to the next within a wink.

The most sensational headline that day concerned Daniel Goodwin, who climbed the side of the Sears Tower dressed as Spiderman. They should have grabbed hold of my story instead: *Woman from future travels to past on subway and is confronted by her deceased relatives. Film at eleven.*

I decided to take a stroll around the neighborhood while I waited for the barbecue to start.

I walked around the block and snuck up on my old grammar school. The brick building brought with it many memories, and not all pleasant.

My first day of kindergarten had me in tears when my mother failed to pick me up on time. Sadie would get me thereafter since my parents worked until six, but my mother vowed she would be there on that first day.

"Your mommy is on her way, I promise," my teacher Mrs. Rand said. Her soothing voice did little to sustain the panic rippling my body.

"I'm right here, honey," Mom said when she arrived to find me trembling. "Mommy's right here. I would never leave you."

"Yeah, right!"

By noon I was in my old backyard. The family swarmed around the table: Sadie and the usual suspects, and two of my grandmother's other brothers Tony, Ronnie and Ronnie's wife Maggie. Nobody made an effort to introduce me to the others, because I had apparently met them at some point. A year had gone by in their time, but only a day in mine.

The picnic table sat underneath the green awning with a set of colored lights attached at each corner. Grandma and Uncle Albert took turns grilling burgers. Mom joined them to make sure her burger was, as she liked to say, "burnt." Just the opposite of Dad, who liked his burger pink, like the cow brushed by the candle pink.

The others congregated around the table spooning salads onto their paper plates. My father filled a Styrofoam cup with his drug of choice – coffee.

The child raced around the yard on her red and yellow Big Wheel. She shot a cap gun into the air. A black cowboy hat sheltered most of her head. She pointed the gun at my back.

"Bang."

Little Brat.

Topics ranging from the upcoming wedding of Charles and Diana to the rivalry between Alexis and Krystle on *Dynasty* were discussed as we ate. But it was the Brooklyn expressions I hadn't heard in years that retained my interest: Burgers were made from chop meat, not ground beef. Cream rinse indicated conditioner. Heroes for hoagies. Johnny Pumps were fire hydrants. Stooping meant sitting on the front porch talking to neighbors. And egg crèmes weren't really made from eggs.

Uncle Tony cut into the round sausage – chivalade – as he called it, and shoved it into his face using his fork like a shovel. Sadie flinched, undoubtedly worried that he would choke to death. And with a loaded mouth Uncle Tony asked, "You got any Goombahs in the area?"

"For God's sake, Tony," Grandma implored, "she told you a while ago that her family isn't from here. Mind your damn business."

"Awlright. Fuggedaboudit," Uncle Tony hollered before letting out an obnoxious belch that caused Aunt Elizabeth to squirm in her seat.

"Look at her," Uncle Tony said, "she thinks who the hell she is."

"There's nothing wrong with manners," Aunt Elizabeth shot back.

It wasn't long before the conversation took a turn for the worse after a fight ensued between Uncle Albert and Uncle Tony concerning their rivalry baseball teams: Yanks vs. Mets. "Gaw head!" roared Uncle Albert, who by now had too many beers in him, "The Mets will never be half the team the Yankees are."

Uncle Tony's wide legs pushed at the table every time he got excited. "Who the hell you talking about?" His napkin was still attached to his shirt like a bib; niblets from his corn on the cob flew from the napkin onto Aunt Elizabeth's dish, at which point she jumped up and yelled for them to sit down and behave themselves. Grandma warned her Yankee loving brother to stop drinking or else.

Everyone knew Uncle Albert had a drinking problem except me. Blinded by some form of ignorance, I had downplayed his drinking as a kid. Even the time he played catch with me when I was seven. I threw the ball and he tipped over backwards into the bushes. I thought he was just clumsy.

It was all so much easier when it didn't make sense.

After cannoli, strudel, and three kinds of Italian cookies, I wondered where my mother had gone. She finished her dinner and made room for a few cookies before leaving the table.

I excused myself and told my family I had to stretch. Far better than revealing that I wanted to search for my mother. Even in a moment's absence I found myself missing her.

She was seated on the porch steps, staring ahead at the white picket fence, a look of sadness written across her face.

"There you are!" I said, startling her.

"Yeah, I needed a break from my uncles. They're a little loud in case you haven't noticed."

I sat down just as two stray cats made their way underneath the gate and onto the porch. "Is everything OK?"

"Just thinking."

"About?"

"I'm not sure if you know, but I was adopted."

I knew.

"Anyway, my biological father left when I was an infant. Apparently, my mother couldn't afford to raise me on her own, so she put me up for adoption. She died of pancreatic cancer not long after. My father's living somewhere in The Bronx. I thought about writing him many times. But I guess if he wanted to he would have tried to contact me.

"How does Flo feel about you contacting him?" I asked.

"She doesn't like the idea."

With my attention on my mother's dilemma, a stray cat purred against my back. My body leapt as my legs jutted out from under me.

Unaware of my sudden jolt, my mother did something out of character. She began to weep, an emotion reserved for fragile, more mortal human beings. I knew my mother as a pillar of strength. Yet beneath that sturdy exterior lived a woman capable of weakness.

"Why are you crying?"

"It would have been nice to know my real parents."

I understood the throes of wanting to know a nonexistent parent whose blood coursed your veins. What I couldn't deal with, though, were my mother's tears.

"It's OK," I answered. But it wasn't. The sight of my mother's unraveling emotions produced in me discomfort. Her human side was a stark contrast to the fictitious mother I had created in my mind. I wanted to embrace her, but I didn't know how, because I was the one who needed to be embraced.

"You know, I used to have a brooch that belonged to my real mother. The adoption agency gave it to Flo for me. I wore it for the first time when I graduated high school and never took it off. A year after Frank and I were married, I wore it on the Ferry, but when I leaned over the side of the boat, the brooch slipped off into the water."

"How devastating," I replied, thinking about her ring drifting through the sewer. "Now you don't have any association with your mother."

"Well, that's how I felt at first. But then I got thinking. There has to be something more significant between two people than a piece of jewelry, right?"

We fell silent for several minutes, neither of us knowing what to say until the family decided the barbecue was over. Everyone was tired and wanted to settle in for the evening. The child ran from the yard and hopped into my mother's arms.

When I reached for my mother's hand, the child knocked it away.

"Rebecca," my mother warned. "Don't ever do that again."

My lips curled around my teeth. There was a sense of entitlement in the child, who thought she could claim my mother as her own.

The evening couldn't have been more peaceful, until the stranger made his cameo. I wasn't going to run, not again. If my fear continued he would prey on that weakness until I surrendered.

"Stop following me!" I demanded.

"Do what you came to do."

I spun around and raising my voice said, "You need to go."

The stranger kept his composure. "You came here to release your pain not to reside in it."

I started to walk away, but the stranger continued with his homily.

"Rebecca, I saw your reaction when your mother cried."

"So, what?"

"She's more human than you remember. Flawed with pain and tears."

"My mother is exactly how I remember."

The stranger rubbed the back of his neck. "How can you say that? You saw your mother through the eyes of a child. You knew the mother not the woman?"

I was angered that the stranger knew my thoughts without having told him. "How do you know these things? Who are you?"

"I'm the soft whisper you chose to ignore most of your life. But you must listen now, Rebecca."

Leaning against a telephone pole my eyes converged with the stranger's. "I'm not leaving."

"If you choose to stay, you'll be putting your future at risk."

"I can make things better."

"By remaining a prisoner of the past and holding your family hostage?" the stranger exclaimed in a huff.

"No, by setting things right."

"Everything happened the way it was meant to."

"So I'm just supposed to let my mother die again? Not a chance."

"You can't stop the hands of fate, Rebecca."

Anger coasted through my body like a demon. I shuffled toward my apartment, but one crucial question remained.

"Since you seem to know everything, perhaps you can tell me how I got from 1980 to 1981?"

The stranger stared at me unforgivingly. "That's what you've been doing all along, isn't it? Reliving each year of your childhood? This time, though, you won't be able to edit your memories to reflect only the happy ones."

And with those words he faded into the night.

Ten

Nineteen Eight-Two.

Morning came without warning and a new year was on the horizon. I opened the front door to see *The Daily News* sticking out of the mailbox with a note from Mrs. Russo. "I'm done with the paper. Thought you'd like to read it. Don't be late for work. You know how Mr. Ricci gets if his employees are not at the store by nine."

Mr. Ricci was the most patient man on earth, a saint.

I had just enough time to wash up and have something for breakfast. I removed a box of cereal from the cabinet and stuck it under my right arm, then grabbed a bowl and the carton of milk. I positioned myself at the table and poured out a bowl of Cornflakes. The milk splashed at my face, blending within the pores of my colorless skin.

The year 1982 seemed vague. I couldn't remember specifics, except for my mother taking me to see *Annie* multiple times.

No matter. Everything would change despite the stranger's warning not to disturb forthcoming events.

I couldn't wipe my mother's tears from my mind. It may have been too late for her to know her biological mother but not her father. So I made a brash decision.

The telephone lay a few inches from the couch. Underneath it a phonebook. Looking back, it wasn't my finest moment. But sometimes the heart leads us to places we might otherwise never journey.

His name was Lorenzo Greco. I picked up the phone and listened for a dial tone. The tip of my index finger slipped into the hole of the rotary dial. I rotated the dial clockwise, then repeated the process until I'd used all seven numbers.

It took five rings before the uneven voice on the other end groaned, "Yeah?"

"Lorenzo Greco?"

"Who the hell is this?"

Deep breaths. "You don't know me, but I'm calling about your daughter."

"My what?" His agitated manner was a cue for me to hang up. I should have. I didn't.

"Sir, you and your late wife had a daughter, correct?"

"Listen, I don't know who the hell this is, but you have a nerve. How dare you call me! I ought to…"

I cut Lorenzo, my grandfather, off before finding out what he 'ought to.'

"Sir, hear me out. Your daughter wants a relationship with you. Please, can't you find it in your heart to talk to her?"

The phone slammed down just about rupturing my eardrum. I would have called him back, but fear – or was it regret? – prevented me.

I tried to put my grandfather out of my thoughts and went to the closet to pick out an outfit for work. I decided on a pair of black slacks, a white blouse that buttoned up the front and tied around the waist, with puffy ruffles that were meant to be sleeves.

There was a vanity in the bathroom complete with cosmetics, which I chose to ignore. I didn't wear makeup, and I wouldn't start by slapping war paint onto my face to coincide with the horrid look of the eighties. My face stayed its natural pale color, as opposed to the luminous colors worn by other women: cheekbones accentuated by hot pink rouge; eyelids highlighted with smoky fuchsia or light blue; fake eyelashes; lips bleeding bright red. Every woman in the eighties looked as though they worked for Ringling Brothers.

Avenue U was energetic. Morning commutes in Brooklyn were equivalent to ones in Manhattan. Car horns jammed the air. Citizens shouted. Mothers pulled at their kids, complaining they'd be late for school.

I relished seeing friendly establishments. Through the window of Del Prio's Bakery, I viewed a plethora of deliciousness: Italian wedding cookies, cannoli with white creamy filling, the outer shell sprinkled in powdered sugar. Down the block, Salvadore's Pizzeria, home to the best pizza and Italian Ice. Bennie's Fruit and Vegetable Stand across the street, where occasional punks would lift an apple or two when no one was looking.

A green and yellow striped awning dropped below a vertical white plank with the words Bargain Town spattered across. I smiled at the mechanical horse in front of the store, recalling the numerous times I'd ridden it.

I looked around to see if anyone was watching, then my left leg flew over the horse, both feet inserted in stirrups. I grabbed the horn on the saddle and began to ride.

Through the window I saw Mr. Ricci's full-bodied figure and balding head. "Get in here!" he mouthed. And when I obeyed, he met me with a cantankerous salutation. "You're just about late!" Mr. Ricci's right foot tapped in tempo with the finger he wagged in my face. This wasn't the Mr. Ricci I knew.

"Well, do you need an engraved invitation?" he bellowed. "Go to the storeroom, unpack the boxes and start stocking the shelves."

Behind the register a woman with teased hair and bangle bracelets jingling around her wrists ushered me to the store-room. "What do I do in here?" I wondered aloud.

She looked at me the way everyone did when I was supposed to know something but did not – like a squirrel who'd lost its nut. "Unpack the boxes and put the stuff on the shelves," she urged.

Mr. Ricci's arrogance dumbfounded me. Sadie had brought me into the store numerous times, and Mr. Ricci was always hospitable.

The past didn't exist like it did in my memories. And it was discouraging.

The cashier's name was Dawn. I found that out when she brought an apron to wrap around my ugly clothes and I looked at her name tag. I did recollect the young woman from childhood, all but her name.

Dawn snapped her gum as she helped me unload water pistols and puzzles. I glanced at her face. *Way too much makeup.* Clowns popping out of a car made me giggle.

"Wha?" Dawn asked. At least, it sounded like a question.

"Nothing," I replied and continued to stack shelves with the latest gadgets.

I started fiddling with a Rubik's Cube that fell out of its package. I never could work the 3-D puzzle no matter how many times I twisted it.

With my attention focused on finding the right combination, I hadn't noticed customers coming and going. But the heavy clacking of heels belonged to one customer I couldn't ignore.

"Hello," my mother called out. She had on a beige skirt with a white polka dot blouse covered beneath a belted suit jacket. Her shoulders were straight and firm, thanks to the shoulder pads. I remembered the red leather imitation handbag she squeezed between her pudgy fingers.

"Oh, hello, Ann. What are you doing here?"

"I needed a few odds and ends, so I thought I'd stop by on my way to work. I'm a little late today. Becky wasn't feeling well this morning and didn't want me to leave."

Seeing my mother brought a serenity that I didn't want to end. I was growing desperate to spend every waking moment with her. But there were obstacles. The child. Even when she wasn't around she was always part of the conversation.

I used the opportunity to invite Mom to lunch, just the two of us without any interruptions.

"I brought my lunch today," she replied, much to my letdown. She noticed a look of disappointment written across my face, and after a brief deliberation, reconsidered.

"Of course. We can go to Salvadore's for a slice of pizza."

"Terrific!" I rejoiced.

I stocked shelves and swept floors until the hour struck noon, at which point I threw down my apron and hitched the broom in a corner and journeyed over to Salvadore's.

Inside, I found my mother already seated. "How's work?" she asked as I sat opposite her.

Bargain Town enticed me more when I could shop for toys, rather than setting them on shelves.

"I guess it's OK. But Mr. Ricci can be cranky."

My mother laughed. "Yeah, he has his moments. Sadie brings my daughter there a lot. Mr. Ricci is always nice to her and she adores him. You'd never know he hates children."

I could feel my eyes widen. "He hates children?"

"Sure. Everyone in Sheepshead Bay knows that."

I couldn't be sure how evident my shock appeared when the waiter came to take our order.

"I'll have two slices with pepperoni," my mother said without looking at the menu. "And bring us a pitcher of Coke."

"And for you?" asked the waiter

"I'll have the same." It had been too long since I tasted Salvadore's round, gooey pizza. As a kid, the cheese would get caught in my throat until I was forced to pull it out with my fingers. I thought I'd die a few times. But what a way to go.

We spoke about the latest fashion trends, which I found repulsive and my mother found hip. She hadn't emerged from the eighties, so she didn't know any better.

Throughout the conversation she seemed distracted, almost troubled. Switching places was awkward. She hadn't been there to console me during the trying times in my life. But there I was reaching out to her. It was unnatural.

"Is anything wrong?" I probed.

The waiter brought our pizza to the table. Steam saturated the air while the edges of each slice slithered off paper plates.

Mom took two bites before returning the pizza to the plate. "I got an unexpected call early this morning from my biological father."

Cheese stormed down my throat, at which point I grabbed the pitcher of Coke and poured half a glass, then took a few sips until my throat cleared. The heat from the cheese penetrated the pit of my stomach.

"Your father!" I said when all was clear. "What did he want?"

"Well, I thought he wanted to talk. That's what he said at first. Took a few minutes to know he just wanted to con me out of money."

I couldn't move. What had I done?

"It's odd that my father called. It sure caused a ruckus between me and my mother, though. She thought I got in touch with him."

"I'm so sorry," I stuttered while my body swelled with guilt.

My intention was to help my mother reunite with her long lost father, but the result didn't pan out that way.

Quickly she changed the subject. "Let's talk about something else. Tell me about back home. Any friends?"

As I moved cubes of ice around the plastic cup with my straw, I said, "Jen was my best friend."

"Was? Past tense?"

"Yeah, she got rid of me when she got married."

"I see," my mother declared. "And that bothers you, doesn't it?"

I spit a chunk of ice into the cup where it crashed against flowing waves of brown liquid.

"Yeah, it bothers me. She ditched me."

My mother dabbed part of her napkin in a glass of water and wiped at the grease stain on her blouse.

"Don't be discouraged. Her life just moved in another direction. It happens. My best friend felt the same way after I married Frank."

I couldn't believe her confession. Had she ditched her friends?

"Antonia was my best friend since grammar school. She didn't like it when I married Frank because my time wasn't devoted to her anymore. Sometimes our paths carry us to different places. No one's to blame. It's all part of life's cycle, right?"

I bowed my head. My mother seemed assured that change wasn't bad. But me, I didn't believe it.

"Tell me something," Mom said, "your parents are gone, aren't they? I know you don't like to discuss your family, but I think it might help."

Behind my soft grin, alarm. How could I discuss my mother's own death with her? I squirmed and plucked at my bulky clothes.

"Yes," I answered with hesitance. "My mother left."

"You mean died?"

I stopped to consider the difference. Died. Left. It was all the same, wasn't it?

"Yeah."

"Do you remember much about her?"

What did I know about someone who'd been part of my life for nine short years? She loved Donald Duck and Miss Piggy; Perry Como and Elvis; *Gone with the Wind* and *The King and I*; she loved sauce on pizza but not pasta; she drank tea instead of coffee.

"Not much, I'm afraid."

"Well," she said, "I'm sure your mother is very proud of the woman you've become."

The woman I'd become? I hadn't done anything that would have caused pride in my mother. My life was rooted in dejection.

"Were you close to your father?"

I thought for a moment. "He never let anyone get too close to him when I was younger."

"Sounds like my Frank," Mom replied.

"Yeah. He came out of his shell after my mother died, then I got to know him better."

My mother smiled. "But your mother's the one you feel you never knew, right?"

"I knew the mother not the woman. There's a big difference."

"And you haven't moved on yet?"

"How can I?"

"I know if something were to happen to me I would want my little Becky to go on with her life."

Something was brewing in my mother's brain, this I knew by the contorted look on her face.

"What's wrong?" I asked.

"Oh, it's Becky. She's been acting different. Always asking me if I'm going to die. God forbid I have a cold, she thinks I'm dying. The other day during my nap, she ran over and pulled up one of my eyelids. I asked her what she was doing, and she said, 'Just checking.'"

My heart missed a beat. All the air in the room abruptly dissolved. I leaned over the table and panted like a dog back from a long run. Mom called out to the waiter for a paper bag, then she held it to my face until it palpitated.

"Are you OK?" she asked.

"Fine," I replied, taking a sip of soda. "Why do you think she's doing those things?"

"Becky? I have no idea. I keep telling her I'm not going anywhere."

Junior high. High school. Puberty. Confirmation. Graduation. My first boyfriend. First apartment. No mother. I'd been dependent on photos and videos and other mothers to bring me the comfort that should have come from her.

I let out a heavy sigh and rested my head against the wall.

"I'm sorry," she said in a panic. "I shouldn't be talking about this with you."

"Dad used to tell me I was the daughter my mother always wanted. So where has she been all these years?"

My mother leaned over the table and took my face in her hands. "It's not about the amount of time you spend with someone."

After lunch, I had to get back to work quickly before Mr. Ricci criticized me for being late. I thanked my mother for the pizza, which she had magnanimously paid for.

"My pleasure," she said. "Darn it. I forgot Becky's notebook. I'll drop by the drugstore on my way home from work."

"Does she need it for school?" I asked.

"No. She likes to write in them, even though at her age she can't write much. She draws pictures, puts down a few words, and calls them her stories. I think she's meant to be a writer."

"Do you want her to be a writer?" I asked.

"That would be something. I just hope she gets over her hatred of school and goes to college someday."

"I never went to college," I added. "It's too late for that now, I guess."

"It's never too late," Mom said. "The only time life stops is when you die."

Eleven

Nineteen Eighty-Three.

Sundays meant no work. I squeezed into my jeans, threw on a t-shirt, and went on the prowl for a bag of bagels. "Only half," I told myself after finding them in the breadbox.

I turned on a small radio above the sink. My left cheek swelled with a chunk of bagel; sesame seeds popped from my jaws as I lip synched to a song until a commercial took its place. I had the attention span of a knat but managed to hear bits of dialogue. Something to do with a guide of some sort.

"That's right," I heard one man say, "we all have one, but not everyone acknowledges them."

The conversation picked up when another guy asked, "How come I don't see mine?"

"Because there's nothing to see. They come in subtle ways like a silent whisper. The more intuitive you are, the more apt you are to pay attention."

With a click of a knob I turned off the radio. *Guides. Intuition. The unconscious.* Irrelevant babble.

The sky was devoid of sun. A stale, damp odor pervaded the air. Mrs. Russo peeked out the window and aimed her triangular chin at me. "Have a good day," she hollered as I rushed off the stoop. I wiggled my fingers rather than wave and kept my focus on the path to my grandmother's.

I arrived to hear voices evolving from the backyard, a conversation between Mom and Grandma. I lingered by the garden to listen.

"Frank doesn't even try anymore," Mom said.

Grandma tried to ease her daughter's worries. "Ann, marriage isn't easy, you have to work at it."

"Ma, I have been. It's a two-way street, you know."

A twig cracked underneath my shoe informing both ladies that they had company. "Hi, come on back," Mom said in her inviting tone.

I searched my memory for images of marital troubles between my parents, but I could locate none.

Grandma had heard enough, leaving us to mingle amongst ourselves.

"Don't mind her," said my mother, cleaning the picnic table with a yellow sponge.

"Ann, you and Frank never gave the impression that anything was wrong between the two of you."

"Every marriage has difficulties." Mom detected my discomfort by my poor posture. "Are you OK?" she asked.

In a monotone voice, I replied, "I'm fine."

"I know he loves me," my mother whispered. "He just doesn't show it. He's withdrawn much of the time. I suppose that happens after you've been together for so long."

Mom's eyes brimmed with tears, giving me a second glimpse at the unfamiliar woman.

"Don't worry, Ann," I said, laying her head on my shoulder. "Everything will work out for the best."

Mom didn't know I was older than her. That in 2009, I had less than a month before turning thirty-four, while she remained thirty-three. It wasn't natural. I had to stop her death before we traded places permanently.

My grandmother opened the kitchen window and stuck her head out. "You've got a call, Ann."

Inside the hallway my mother leapt up the stairs two at a time, with no regard that our time together had been interrupted again. I curled my fist and beat it against the wall.

Aunt Bernice opened her door on the third thump. "Well, look who it is! Hello, dear."

My voice dropped as I inquired, "Would you mind some company?"

"Not at all," she said in her merry way.

"Come on in," said Aunt Elizabeth. "I'm making an afghan."

I lowered myself beside her on the couch. Sandy took his usual spot alongside Aunt Bernice's leather recliner. She reached over to pet him. "That's my baby," she said to her furry companion as he wagged his tail.

Judy Garland's *Over the Rainbow* resounded from the large stereo propped against the wall.

"Would you like something cold to drink?" Aunt Bernice offered to which I accepted.

She returned with a mug of club soda for herself and a tall glass of ginger ale for me, bubbles hissing symphonically as she placed the glass atop the marble coffee table.

Unlike other homes whose interior exhibited dull colors, my aunts' added flash to their décor. The original brown carpeting had been torn up and replaced by a burgundy color. The couch had a flowery red and gold pattern beneath its plastic covering. Beside the television was a black imitation fireplace. Much of the walls were paneled, complete with artwork they'd had done of Sandy when he was a puppy. White appliances filled the kitchen and light green curtains hung over the windows. The kitchen table was embedded in the corner of the wall, resembling a countertop more than a table.

"Sweetheart," Aunt Elizabeth said, breaking my train of thought. "Ann told us about your parents."

"I'm sorry, what?" I asked, feeling embarrassed about being caught off guard.

"We know your parents are gone," Aunt Bernice added.

"Yes, they are." I was hopeful that the conversation would drop. But my aunts never left anything unresolved.

"Are you happy in Brooklyn?" Aunt Bernice chimed in.

How could I not be happy spending time with family and getting acquainted with the mother I'd been forced to live without? But my heart belied feelings of contentedness. The past was not the idyllic place I'd reminisced about.

"Everything is fantastic," I lied as the aunts looked on.

Aunt Elizabeth steadied her gaze on me. "We've noticed how attached you are to Ann."

"She's like a mother to me."

"You remind me so much of Becky," Aunt Elizabeth exclaimed, "the way you cling to her."

The comparison offended me. "There's nothing wrong with looking at Ann as a mother," I responded in defense.

"I disagree, sweetheart."

Dumbfounded. That's what I was sitting alongside the aunt who'd been my hero.

I shouldn't have said it, but it came out nonetheless.

"What if I never see Ann again? I can't live with that." Both aunts stopped what they were doing. Down went the mug of club soda and the needle and thread. Even Sandy lifted his wet snoot.

I gave my aunts everything I had. "Just like that everyone disappears; the sound of their voice, the light in their eyes, the smile you come to depend on. All that's left is a name etched in stone."

"Sweetheart, I know you miss your mother, but clinging to Ann won't bring her back. You will never find closure if you don't give your mother to God."

Give my mother to God? She belonged to me. Aunt Elizabeth had no right to ask me to give up my own mother.

After another sip of club soda Aunt Bernice said, "Don't you ever think about going back home?"

I choked down a sob. Brooklyn was my home. They were trying to get rid of me; trying to send me back to a time and place I didn't belong.

"My life was miserable back there," I began. "I was all alone. I broke up with my boyfriend, then I changed my mind. But he wouldn't come back."

"Was he good to you?" Aunt Bernice inquired.

"He cheated on me, so I broke up with him."

I should have predicted what Aunt Elizabeth would say next. "He cheated on you, yet you wanted him back? What on earth for?"

"Better than being alone."

"I was married once," Aunt Bernice professed. "It didn't last long. I left and started a new life. Never looked back."

"You can't run from your problems, sweetheart."

"That's right," Aunt Bernice replied as she reached over to stroke Sandy's back.

"Why does everyone want to push me away?" I responded.

Aunt Elizabeth shifted on the couch. "Sweetheart, I don't believe when you came to Brooklyn it was supposed to be permanent. Seems to me like you're running from something."

I shook my head.

"We just want what's best for you. We won't be around much longer."

"You won't?" I asked panic-stricken.

Aunt Bernice laid her mug on the end table. "We're thinking about retiring to Florida. As a matter of fact, we're going there on vacation in a few weeks to look at homes."

"That's right. We've been saving for the trip."

I knew the story well, how my aunts saved three-thousand dollars and hid the money underneath Aunt Elizabeth's mattress because they didn't trust banks.

But if everyone stayed in Brooklyn, if my mother didn't have to die, well, then everything would be perfect.

Two mistakes in one night, that's what happened. Aunt Elizabeth passed a green thread through the eye of her crocheting needle. "Do you have any writing paper?" I inquired.

"Do you want to write a letter, sweetheart? Maybe to someone back home?"

"Yes, please." I was aware of the writing desk in Aunt Elizabeth's bedroom, an antique Victorian roll top where she wrote her most intimate letters. "May I have a few pieces to take with me?"

"Nonsense. You go right to the bedroom on the left and write your letter at my desk. Here I'll show you."

Aunt Bernice stooped down to give Sandy a belly rub while I followed Aunt Elizabeth to her room.

"Please excuse the towels. Albert was down here earlier fixing the air conditioner."

She waited until I sat down before handing me a stack of multi-colored stationary. Then she took her exit, closing the door halfway.

Left alone, the future was mine to salvage. The money rested underneath the mattress, but that would have to wait, for I had other business that needed tending first.

Something needed to be done to save my parents' marriage. But Dad wasn't one to talk about his personal life, so with pen in hand, I wrote him an anonymous letter.

Dear Frank,

It appears that you and Ann are not happy, and I can't tell you how much that saddens me. You can overcome these unfortunate circumstances by being more attentive, by giving more of your soul to your soulmate. You may think me out of line for saying so, but we share much in common, concealed within a sturdy shell where those on the outside can all but see in. Give Ann the opportunity to know the man inside.

I folded the letter and shoved it inside an envelope, then wrote my father's name across the front. Though my writing mirrored that of his chicken scratch, he wouldn't recognize my conspicuous penmanship.

And that's when the second mistake took place. I peeped through the door to make sure my aunts were nowhere in sight before lifting the mattress and finding three thousand dollars inside a business envelope.

Shoulders tense, I nabbed the envelope, lifted my shirt, and wedged it in my pants before rejoining my aunts.

"Thanks for the writing paper," I said.

Aunt Elizabeth opened the door and rested her hand on my shoulder. "Just remember, sweetheart, better days are coming."

I stuck the letter in the mailbox knowing my father rooted through the mail before anyone else.

The usual commotion of neighbors trading gossip on their front stoops and cars hammering the street dwindled. A hundred thoughts pounded my mind. What would my father do when he read the letter? What would my aunts do once they discovered the missing money? It wasn't meddling if you had someone's best interest at heart. Was it?

Inside my bedroom, I combed through my backpack for my journal, pushing aside the urn containing my father's remains. Journaling was not new to me. I'd been a friend for years, a cathartic way to sort out my thoughts without judgment.

The harsh bedpost nudged my spine as I composed the journal over my lap. Pressing down on the pencil, I began to write until the tip could no longer sustain pressure from my finger. I went for a pen, then filled two pages with the day's events.

The raucous sound of the telephone drew me from my thoughts. My mother's voice sounded from the other end.

"It's Frank," she said unable to capture a breath. "He walked out on me."

The letter meant to rectify my parents' marriage had torn it asunder. I calmed my mother before inquiring the facts.

"Frank got this anonymous letter telling him to work on our marriage. He said I should have kept my mouth shut instead of blabbing our business to everyone. Who could have sent it? Only a few people know about our problems."

Everything turned upside down. My mother felt betrayed by my father; my father by my mother. And both had been betrayed by their daughter.

"He told me if I'm that miserable he'd leave."

I'd never heard my mother so frantic. In my endeavor to save my parents' marriage, I had severed it.

"He'll come back," I reassured her. "Everything will work out."

"I hope you're right," she muttered.

Of all my father's endearing qualities, forgiveness was his strongest trait. He was quick to anger, slow to heal. But always forgiving.

"Do you know where he might have gone?"

"Probably the movies. That's where he always goes when he wants to be alone."

"He'll be back, trust me." I hung up the phone and hoped for the best.

The stranger entered my apartment out of nowhere with his arms crossed. He didn't say a word at first. I stood ahead of him guarding myself against his accusatory glare. Then I gave it to him. "I know why you're here."

He unfolded his arms and crept closer. "What is it going to take to make you realize what you're doing to yourself? To your family?"

Heat generated inside of me, a sign that my blood pressure was on the rise. "I'm just trying to fix things."

The stranger sat down like an invited guest. "You're trying to fix what isn't broken."

I laughed out loud. "I'm not about to allow my parents to have problems."

"Your parents were still together when your mother died, so they worked things out, yes?"

"My mother deserves to be happy all the time," I screamed until my voice was hoarse.

The stranger stood like a soldier marching off to battle.

"Your mother's illness brought them closer." He took my hands and held onto them. "Sometimes our most defining moments come at the end."

But there would be no end if I could help it, because my mother would not die. Not this time.

"I can't leave if that's what you're thinking," I moaned, then crouched in a ball. "This is my home."

"This hasn't been your home in many years," insisted the stranger. "You cannot make a life here because none of it is real. The stores you've been to, torn down; the homes in the neighborhood, remodeled; the people you've encountered, dead."

My chest tightened. I concentrated on my enemy. "If nothing is real," I shouted, "then what is this? It's the past. I'm in the past. My past."

"The past only exists when you dwell in it." The stranger moved toward the window. "Don't go on, Rebecca. Free yourself."

"Free myself from what?"

He angled his head sideways.

"Self-destruction."

Twelve

By the time I got to the theater, I'd hardly noticed my father outside propped against a wall, his right foot in a slow tap on the sidewalk. "Oh, where did you come from?" he said, cradling a bucket of popcorn.

"Frank, thank God I found you."

"Why?" he answered, shoving a handful of buttered kernels into his mouth.

"Ann is worried about you, Frank. You have to go back."

"Great, what is she telling the whole world now?"

"It's not like that."

"Well, I'm staying right here, even if I have to sit through five movies."

I scowled at my father, put off by his stubborn personality. "You're running from your problems, Frank."

"Are you some kind of an expert?"

Was I an expert on running away? At the time I didn't think so.

Reaching for some popcorn, I said, "Just sit down with Ann and listen to what she has to say."

"What's the point? Everyone wants to change me."

"They're trying to help you."

"It was better when we first got married. Now Ann's busy working, running to PTA meetings, going to lunch with friends."

I didn't recognize this father, the one who yearned for yesterday. "Things change, Frank. You just have to keep up."

Dad hadn't given up after my mother died, even if it would have been easier. He could have shipped me off to live with my grandmother, have her raise me. But he didn't. He'd cooked and cleaned, attended every back to school night. Holidays and birthdays were always celebrated. A widower by his mid-thirties with a child to raise and a disease to contend with. Yet I never heard him complain. Somewhere he'd found the courage to move on. I wanted that courage. Needed that courage.

"Is Ann that worried?" my father asked.

"Of course she is. She loves you, Frank."

He threw the empty popcorn tub into the trash and wiped his buttery hands on his jeans.

The walk home was quiet, my father's conventional personality trait. Nothing until we reached the house and he lifted his cheek to expose a few teeth. I smiled back and wished him a good night. All would be well.

All would be well.

Thirteen

Nineteen Eighty-Four.

The envelope containing the three thousand dollars lay in the front flap of my bag. I took out the money and counted it, my guilt increasing with the passing of each bill between my clammy fingers. I was not a thief. The stolen money was a desperate appeal to freeze a few moments of time.

My journal sat beside me at the kitchen table while I ate breakfast. I thumbed through the pages, making certain I had chronicled every incident with prudence: the letter to my father, the money, my mother's tears, and the phone call to my grandfather, all positioned on white lined paper.

With the breakfast dishes washed I threw my journal into my backpack and headed to Bargain Town. Mondays were long and busy, breaks at a premium. Although I didn't thrill to the idea of stocking shelves, I needed the money. The cost of living in Brooklyn was on the rise. Another reason my aunts wanted to escape.

I bit my lower lip.

Along the avenue, the smell of warm donuts hung in the air. I stopped in front of Del Prio's Bakery to absorb the pleasurable fragrance. It was the same bakery my father used to bring me to. We'd stray inside and fill a box to take home. Maybe the trips to the bakery had caused my father's health to fail.

Mr. Ricci flashed his favorite mood as I walked through the door, shoving his watch in my face, his green eyes twitching.

"Do you see the time?" he cried. "Two minutes to nine. You know very well I like my employees here fifteen minutes early. One more time and you're outta here."

My hands clenched; my nostrils broadened. The urge to tell Mr. Ricci to go to hell pained me since my memories were of a gentleman and not the bully he kept hidden beneath a veil.

"I'm sorry. It won't happen again," I said before filing into the storeroom.

The past was starting to grate my nerves.

Mr. Ricci had patted my head and pinched my cheeks as a kid, spoke to me in a grandfatherly fashion. "You're such a good girl," he'd say. Mr. Ricci, it seemed, was two people. Maybe we all were.

Dawn brought over my apron. "You OK?" A wad of Juicy Fruit alternated between her left and right jaw.

"Just great," I answered with animosity.

It was a long morning with customers buying and returning. Dawn popped bubbles with her gum and moved her slender fingers across the register like she was playing piano. Mr. Ricci held open the door for ladies with multiple packages. He wore his mask well.

Around eleven, Sadie waltzed in with the child, who was grabbing at her pants. "Hiya, Lynn."

"Hey, what brings you in today?"

"We just came from Salvadore's. Becky had to have a Cherry Italian Ice. Now she can't make it home. I told her to go before we left the pizza parlor, but oh, no."

The child bounced from one leg to the other. Mr. Ricci happened by and told her she could use the toilet in the storeroom. "Show her where it is, Dawn," he said in his affable manner that sounded more like the old Mr. Ricci from my childhood.

Dawn led the way, then returned to her register.

Minutes later the child emerged with her New York Yankee's jacket buttoned to the top.

"Stop by later this evening for some crumb cake," Sadie said.

"Will do," I replied.

Once Sadie had gone, I went to the storeroom for some aspirin to ease the thrashing inside my head. Mr. Ricci made it impossible to relax with his irritating habit of standing guard as I stocked shelves, making sure every item was in its rightful place. Mistakes would be noted.

The medicine cabinet in the restroom was chock full of bottled remedies – cures for everything from allergies to cramps. *I bet Midol wouldn't cure Mr. Ricci's PMS.*

A box of Band-Aids tumbled into the sink as I opened the door. I took the soggy adhesive bandages and positioned them back in their box. Mr. Ricci would notice if one stood above the rest.

I grabbed a bottle of aspirin and went over to the water cooler, filled a cone-shaped cup, then cast two bitter tablets in my mouth.

But something caught my eye.

I curved my head left and that's when I saw it. I dropped the cup from my hand. The remaining water made a small puddle around my feet.

My blue backpack sitting on the stool where I'd thrown it earlier was wide open. I ran over and inspected its contents. "My journal!" I fumbled around until I felt my father's urn. I checked the front pocket containing the envelope of money. Also there. But the journal was gone.

The child.

The zipper on my backpack jammed after a piece of vinyl got caught in its teeth; my fingers tweaked the clasp until it was fastened. And just as I bolted out of the store, Mr. Ricci loudly pronounced that I would be fired if I didn't come back. His threat ricocheted down Avenue U as I ran toward Crestwood.

Red lights didn't deter my small figure from weaving in and out of traffic. Brooklynites leaned on their horns, but the honking had no effect.

The journal could not be opened. Even if the child was too young to understand, what if she showed it to my family? They would call the police, or worse - the lunatic asylum.

In my rush, I forced myself between two teenagers on skateboards, shoving them out of my way. "Jerk!" they screamed.

I hustled past Avenue T where Mrs. Russo rocked a broom on the porch. She waved and called out my name, but I kept in motion. Meg's old house was long behind and Sadie's just seconds away.

Ten minutes gone, leaving me to think the worst.

A crack in the sidewalk sent me straight to the ground where the right side of my cheek skinned the pavement. Fresh blood dripped from my face onto my shirt as I crawled through Sadie's gate, up the steps, and pounded on her door.

"Are you awlright?" Sadie said.

"Where is she?" I implored.

"Who?"

That little brat. "Becky," I answered, trying to replenish the air that had been snuffed from my lungs.

"Oh, oh. Flo got home early."

The nightmare continued, giving the child more time to foil my plans.

"Did they go home?"

"No, no. They went to the drugstore on Kings Highway." Down the stairs, through the gate, I rounded the corner without giving clarification to Sadie.

Avenue S. Nostrand Avenue. Kings Highway. The drugstore was somewhere, but in all the commotion I couldn't pinpoint the exact location.

I snatched the arm of a woman walking by and inquired about its whereabouts. She shrugged me off and kept on her way.

"Where the hell is that drugstore?" I said out loud.

Between a herd of shoppers, Grandma and the child came out of an ice-cream parlor. The child's tongue flew up and down, straining to seize the drops of chocolate ice-cream gliding down her cone.

"Flo!" I cried out.

"Hi," she called back.

The child saw me approaching and hid behind my grandmother.

"I'm sorry to be out of breath. I ran all the way from Avenue U."

"What for?"

"I think Becky has something of mine. A journal." I prayed that Grandma would investigate the child's coat, which was still buttoned to the top; a small bulge protruding beneath the fabric.

"Becky, do you have something that doesn't belong to you? You'd better tell me or you're in big trouble, girly," my grandmother reprimanded.

The child shoved the last of the cone into her mouth and took off her coat. The journal was pressed against a blue cut off shirt, reminiscent of the off the shoulder shirt worn in the movie *Flashdance*. In the center, the word *Maniac* was written crossways.

"I don't believe you!" Grandma scolded. "You never take anything that's not yours. I'm so disappointed."

As her words flowed, I reflected on what my grandmother would say if she knew about the money.

"It's not her fault," I interrupted. "I told her she could have one of my notebooks, and she must have taken the wrong one by mistake."

Grandma apologized profusely, after which she asked if I would watch the child while she went into the drugstore. I agreed. It would give me an opportunity to probe the child about the journal.

When my grandmother was out of sight, I took the child by the shoulders; she stared blankly into my eyes. "Did you open my journal and read it?" I inquired.

No answer.

"It's very important that I know. Did you read my journal?"

Still, no answer.

"DID YOU READ IT?" my voice climbed, sending the child running inside the drugstore and me sailing after her.

I clipped the child's jacket and pulled her to the side before she could find my grandmother, who was standing in line at the other end of the store.

"I'll ask again. Did you read it?"

"I don't like you," the child exclaimed, scrunching her nose at me.

"Do you think I care how you feel about me?"

The child took a Slinky from its box and jiggled the spring in both hands. "She's *my* mommy."

"What are you talking about?"

"You're trying to take my mommy away."

"I deserve to be with her for a change. You're always there, clinging to her like a little brat. What good is your time with her anyway? You won't even remember half of it when you're older."

Words can be harsh often wounding their recipient. The child threw down the Slinky and started to cry.

A biting chill cascaded down my backbone, hindering my speech. There he stood, the stranger, leering at me. Yet he said nothing. Did nothing.

"Come on now," I said, trying to soothe the child. "Don't cry. I didn't mean it." I struggled to dry her tears, but she smacked at my hand and dried them herself.

My grandmother found her way over to us. "Was she any trouble?" she asked.

I bared my teeth. "None whatsoever."

"That's good to hear. She can be a handful sometimes."

You're telling me.

Before taking her leave, Grandma invited me over to her house for dinner and dessert. I revealed that Sadie asked me over for dessert later in the evening, but Grandma said she'd call Sadie and invite her to bring the cake over there instead. We swapped adieus, then she took the child by the hand and walked out of the store, but not before the child turned and stuck out her tongue.

Little brat.

The stranger had also taken his leave.

Above my head a billboard read: Letting Go. I laughed because I knew who'd put it there. The stranger was nothing if not persistent.

I desperately needed sleep but was vigilant not to close my eyes.

I threw my feet, shoes and all, on the coffee table and laid my head back. With the palm of my left hand facing the ceiling, two of my fingers found their way to my wrist and located a slow pulse. The joints in my knees sounded like a rusty hinge at the bend. Even my breathing was shallow. All of my yesterdays were taking a toll. But I would not be defeated.

The phone's persistent ring drove me from the couch. "Hello?" I answered with a yawn.

"Taking chances, aren't we?" said the voice.

"Who is this?"

"It's your friendly wake-up call."

The stranger.

"Sorry, I can't talk right now."

The handset just about hit the base when the stranger demanded, "Don't you dare hang up, Rebecca."

"Look, it's not my fault the little brat is a thief."

The stranger exhaled into the receiver; tiny vibrations prickled my eardrum. "Rebecca, do what you came to do," he suggested.

"Change of plans," I replied with arrogance.

"Did you forget that you got fired? How do you expect to pay bills now?"

"What? Is Bargain Town the only job in Brooklyn?" I answered sarcastically.

"Your time is wearing thin, Rebecca. Tonight when you lay your head to rest, another year will have gone by."

I let out an additional yawn. "So?"

"Are you prepared for the changes that accompany it?"

"I'll fix everything."

"You're not in control, something you have yet to accept. Everything will proceed as planned."

One blow from my shoe sent the phone crashing. A vase shattered against the wall. Feathers from a throw pillow soared through the air as if a bird had been plucked mid-flight.

Mrs. Russo banged on the door; her daily chores suspended by the turmoil taking place inside my apartment.

"What's all the fuss?" she implored when I swung open the door. "What happened in here?"

"I'm sorry," I said. "I knocked over a vase and tripped over the table and the phone fell."

She looked around at the scattered feathers gliding above. With no plausible excuse, I bowed my head, eager for the interrogation to end.

"Try to be more careful," Mrs. Russo cautioned, her index finger shaking opposite me.

Fourteen

Dinner took place at 6:30, but I arrived at my grandmother's ten minutes early, let in by Uncle Albert, who answered the door in blue shorts, white tube socks, and a dirty t-shirt. He never bothered with greetings when the ponies were on, so he told me to close the door and hobbled back to his chair to finish his suds.

Grandma was in the kitchen listening to the radio as she covered ravioli in meat sauce, remembering to set aside some plain pasta for my mother.

The child surfaced from upstairs carrying a box of crayons under one arm, construction paper under the other. She took to the floor and shot me a look. She was up to something, I could feel it. The temperature in my body rocketed as the pages of my journal dominated each thought.

I knelt beside the child, pretending to take interest in her latest artistic creation, but she took her paper and crayons and moved away from me. "What are you drawing?" I gave a smile, a peace offering to earn the child's trust. She flipped the paper toward me. Two people sat in the middle. "Who's that?"

"Me and my mommy." She turned over the construction paper, exposing a third person on a bus with curly hair and a backpack.

Her cheap antics had little bearing on me.

"It's my turn," I answered through clenched teeth.

"Nope," she refuted, shaking her head. "She can't be your mommy."

In a sharp tone I asked, "Why not?"

"Because she's not meant to be your mommy."

Adult to child, we stared one another down, waiting to see who would make the next move.

I heard two sets of footsteps coming up the stairs in the hall. At Uncle Albert's inebriated request, I opened the door and in walked Aunt Elizabeth and Aunt Bernice.

"Well, you made it," Aunt Bernice said with a grin. "Flo told us you were coming over."

"Hello, sweetheart," exclaimed Aunt Elizabeth.

My father was upstairs but could sense when dinner was ready, not by the smell of food, but by the percolating coffee pot. He tore down the stairs like a junkie in need of a fix. My mother waved from behind.

The usual scene took place at dinner: Grandma rebuked Uncle Albert for his drinking; Aunt Elizabeth reprimanded him for his belching. Aunt Bernice told a story about meeting Frank Sinatra when he was still a scrawny nobody from New Jersey. My mother talked about the latest PTA meeting as Dad ingested mouthfuls of coffee, and the child sat on a stool poking her ravioli with a fork until the filling seeped out.

"Mommy," the child called out.

"Yes?" my mother replied, scraping at specks of sauce that blotted her ravioli.

"Can I sit by you, Mommy?"

"No, Becky. We're not playing musical chairs."

She ran over and latched onto my mother.

"What am I going to do with you, huh?" Mom said.

I watched as the child sat on my mother's lap, wondering what it would be like to feel the comfort of my mother's arms wrapped around me instead of my adversary.

Aunt Elizabeth looked over at me. "Did we tell you we found a house in Florida?"

The fork flew from my hand, bouncing on the table past my father's dish.

"Flo loaned us the money. I wish I knew where *our* money went," Aunt Bernice grumbled. "I'm still sick over it."

The money in question was with me. I stole a look at the child, thinking about my journal.

Thief.

Grandma reached for the Italian bread. "Well, who leaves that much money in the house?" she countered.

"Oh, Flo!" added Aunt Elizabeth. "You know how we feel about banks. Anyway, it couldn't have just disappeared."

All eyes turned to Uncle Albert, who had just sat back down with another can of beer.

"Gaw head. You don't think I took the money?"

"Keep quiet," Grandma declared. "Nobody said it was you. But you were in their apartment before it disappeared."

"What's that supposed to mean?" Uncle Albert slammed his can of beer off the table; slices of bread jumped in the wicker basket.

"Don't you slam that can on the table," Aunt Elizabeth reproached.

"A few drinks now and then, trips to the track, and I'm a thief? I suppose I wrote a letter to Frank, too? And maybe it was me who called Ann's bum of a father, how about that?"

"That letter had to come from Crazy Linda," Grandma said to my mother. "Didn't I warn you not to trust her with your business?"

"Well, I didn't take no money," answered Uncle Albert. He folded his arms, refusing to finish his supper. A gambler. Someone who slurred his words when he drank. But a thief he was not.

Ever the peacemaker, my mother calmed the family's frayed nerves. "Nobody's accusing anyone. Let's just have a nice dinner."

I pushed my dinner around the plate. Family gatherings were never tense in the home movies my father had captured with his Super 8.

"Wait a second," said Aunt Elizabeth. "Let's get a picture."

While everyone groaned at my aunt's favorite hobby, I beamed with pride to have a new photo of me with my family, proof that the past was more than just one's imagination.

Aunt Elizabeth pulled a Polaroid out of her purse. "Gather around and smile. Lynn, stand by Ann and Becky." The child snorted and refused to put her arm around my waist; the feeling was mutual.

Smiles. Flash. The photo slid from the camera. Aunt Elizabeth fanned the picture back and forth while I waited in anticipation. My mother returned to her seat to clean off the rest of her ravioli. The child, as always, standing guard at her side.

"What on earth?" said Aunt Elizabeth. "Something went wrong. Everyone came out in the picture except Lynn."

The photo revealed Grandma standing near Uncle Albert, his left arm cradling his overweight stomach. Aunt Bernice was seated in a chair at the table, in back of her were my parents and the child. I was supposed to be on my mother's left, but in my place, a bright light.

"The hell is that?" Uncle Albert implored.

"Let's take another one." Aunt Elizabeth posed us again but had no film left. We returned to our seats and resumed eating.

"Is everything alright?" Mom asked. "You hardly touched your food."

"I'm not feeling very well," I answered.

"Maybe the pasta is too heavy?" muttered my grandmother. "Do you have pain?"

Nausea was more like it. The notion of the trouble I'd brought my family and the possibility of the child having read my journal aggravated my digestion.

"I'll be OK," I said, pushing away my dish after a failed attempt to down another ravioli.

Sadie knocked twice, then let herself in. Two of her fingers were tangled in a string tied around a white bakery box. My father's eyes broadened at the glorious sight.

The family continued their chatter while I remained silent. I had been more generous with dialogue on previous occasions, but my eyes floated from my aunts, who would move away by the year's end, to my father, whose body was about to give up on him, to my mother, whose time was running thin.

The child refused to finish her dinner. Instead, she jumped off my mother's lap onto the floor where her coloring supplies lay. Suddenly, with a brush of her hand she declared, "I have a secret."

My heart went airborne. She couldn't know anything. Not anything of importance.

"What secret?" my mother inquired.

I drew a breath and released it. Fists tight, fingernails digging at my palms. "Yes, what secret?" I queried while the child doodled some gibberish on construction paper.

Everyone just about fell off their seats waiting for this epiphany. Uncle Albert sipped his beer and followed it with a belch that shook Grandma's hair.

Throwing one hand into the air the child pointed at me. "She's trying to steal my mommy."

This time my father spoke up. "Becky, stop the nonsense."

"That's right, Becky," my mother added. "Nobody is trying to take me away from you."

The child wouldn't give up. "And she has a pile of dirt in her bag."

I gripped my throat with both hands. *My father's urn.* That menace had seen my father's urn, and even worse, she'd opened it. What was I to say? That the resilient man sitting at the table, emptying sugar down his esophagus, was nothing more than a mass of ashes that I'd come to spread over my mother's grave?

"Did you go through Lynn's things?" my mother asked the child.

"Why the hell you carrying around dirt? Uncle Albert yelled.

"It's not your business," Aunt Elizabeth called out in my defense.

BELCH.

My mother yelled at the child for going through my bag. I was relieved that she hadn't seen the money; if she had, she said nothing, because she was overcome by tears.

Grandma excused herself to the basement to get a load of laundry from the washer and asked if I would assist her.

"Is everything OK?" Grandma asked, taking a white stained shirt of Uncle Albert's and shaking her head at the perpetual blemish. "You're distracted tonight. Come to think of it, you're distracted a lot these days."

"I'm just confused."

"Oh, about what?"

Grandma had no way of knowing that she would soon wipe blood from her daughter's mouth, brush loose hairs from her shoulders, and watch as her young body withered away. But if I could free my mother from her untimely fate, then my grandmother would be spared unnecessary heartbreak.

"I don't quite know where I belong anymore," I replied after restoring my focus.

Grandma folded the last of the laundry before closing the lid to the washer. "Are you having second thoughts about Brooklyn?"

"I guess I had certain expectations about what life in Brooklyn would be like."

"And it's not what you expected?" said my grandmother, placing the last of the laundry in a bamboo basket.

I thought momentarily. No, Brooklyn wasn't what I'd expected or remembered, not at all. My family argued. Uncle Albert drank and gambled. My parents were not June and Ward Cleaver. I wondered why any of it mattered.

"No, nothing is turning out as planned," I said after a long recess.

"I see," Grandma added. "That's something you'll have to work out for yourself. I know you're lonely," she continued, sitting on a paint bucket that was turned upside down. "You miss them, don't you?"

"Who?" I asked, knowing full well.

"Mommy and Daddy. Oh, I'm sorry. Forgive the way I phrased that. I'm so used to talking to my granddaughter."

You are talking to your granddaughter. I'm here, Grandma, right here.

"I've been feeling out of sorts. Something doesn't feel right." Grandma stared at one of the walls as if hoping to find the answer written across it.

I thumbed at my ear and formed a firm smile. "You don't say."

"Did you ever hear of *Deja vu*? I feel like I'm reliving certain things. It's exhausting."

The *Déjà vu* Grandma felt was my intrusion on the past. "Life is hard enough the first time," she once said.

There was still one question I had to ask, an intrusive query that I knew my grandmother would not like answering.

"Why don't you want Ann to know her biological father?"

Grandma paused by the steps, then sat down. She pressed her lips together and shook her head, testimony of her agitation.

"He's bad news. In and out of jail for drugs and theft."

"Then you were just trying to protect her?"

"I never wanted Ann to know anything about that man. What good would it have done? It's important for people to accept things as they are and move on." Grandma looked my way. "Your cheeks are red?"

I couldn't see the color but I could feel the burn. My sagging arms offered little use when I brought them over to my grandmother for comfort. She presented a faint smile and caressed my hand.

"I guess you did the right thing then," I said, swallowing the lump in my throat.

"Oh, I know I did. Ann had a good childhood and that's what I want her to remember. No need for her to be saddled with things beyond her control."

Uncle Albert yelled down to my grandmother that the kitchen sink had overflowed after he filled it to wash his socks. "For heaven's sake," Grandma said as she hurried up the stairs with her laundry basket.

On the way I stopped by my aunts' apartment, aware of the money in my backpack, which I'd brought with me to the basement because I didn't trust the child. I could hear Aunt Elizabeth's voice ringing through the hallway. She was still at my grandmother's. The apartment was clear, giving me the chance to rectify any misgivings I'd caused. I turned the brass doorknob and pushed. To my relief the door was unlocked.

Inside Aunt Bernice's bedroom was a bookcase packed with her favorite tomes. Old and new, hardcover and paperback. I couldn't very well replace the money underneath Aunt Elizabeth's mattress. So I dived for the leather-bound copy of *Gone with the Wind*, removed the envelope, and placed it between the ashen pages.

I was careful to close the door before going back upstairs. Inside, Sadie was ready to take her leave. She recommended we walk out together.

"Good seeing you both," Mom said, helping Sadie on with her coat.

"Ann," I said, "I know it's late, but would you like to come over my apartment, just for a talk?"

"Oh, I don't think so. I'm tired, and I need to spend some time with Becky."

The child occupied my mother's right hand. "Mommy is staying with me," she said.

My throat let out a slim growl. I extended my arm and took my mother's free hand, mimicking that of my rival.

"Are you sure you won't change your mind?" I begged.

The child yanked my mother in her direction and I pulled back until we were involved in a tug of war. She needed her; I needed her more. She had her; I had lived without her for twenty-four years.

One of us had to let go.

Mom withdrew both arms. "What on earth are you both doing?" She shook her head in disapproval without saying anything more. The child stomped off, but I remained at a stiff stance.

"I'm sorry, Ann."

Out came a quiet sigh. "I think we should call it a night."

Grandma's ravioli began to swirl around my stomach. I hung my head low, offering more apologies. My mother would have none of it.

Sadie held onto my arm as I walked her home on that moonless night. Conversation was light, since I had deeper issues on my mind rather than what was going on in the neighborhood.

"We're all worried about you," Sadie said, after reaching her stoop.

"Everything's fine," I muttered.

One question remained, however paranoid it may have been.

"Did that kid read my journal?"

Sadie shuffled back a step or two with an open mouth. "What journal?"

I did my best to regain my composure. Sadie didn't know the child had taken my private thoughts.

"Never mind."

Down the dimly lit block, I heard someone call my name. I was relieved to see Aunt Elizabeth sitting in a chair on her patio with Aunt Bernice not far off, patting Sandy, referring to him as her macho man.

"Sweetheart," Aunt Elizabeth began, "you'll never guess what happened? We found the money!"

Aunt Bernice heaved her lanky body out of the chair. "And you'll never guess where we found it? In a book." She began to laugh. "I said to Elizabeth, I'm in the mood to read on the patio, so I went for my copy of *Gone with the Wind*. How I love that book. I've read it dozens of times, and the movie, oh, what a movie."

"We must have put the money in the book and forgot," Aunt Elizabeth reciprocated. "Never done that before. That's why we never thought to look there in the first place."

I told them how happy I was that they were leaving, lying through my teeth.

"Feeling any better, sweetheart? You didn't look good at dinner."

"Not really. This place is getting to me."

"Well, sweetheart, when you decide you've had enough and long to take back your life, know that we're always with you."

I loitered a few minutes longer, watching as Aunt Elizabeth watered her plants and Aunt Bernice read her book. By morning my aunts would be lounging in the warm Florida rays, and I would never see them again in this lifetime.

There was nothing to do except leave them to their appointed fate.

Fifteen

Inside the large cathedral, a bevy of grievers in black garments assembled in their pews. White linen swathed the rose-colored coffin in front of the altar, while the priest swung a thurible in the air. Unknowing of who lay inside, I looked around to see my grandmother holding a silk handkerchief to her face. Aunt Elizabeth's and Aunt Bernice's hollowed cheeks flushed; dark rings shaped the base of their eyes.

Two figures dropped to their knees by the coffin; my father stoically fixed his gaze on the crucifix hanging on a neighboring partition, while my mother moaned until her resonant voice yielded to the strain.

"Oh, Becky, you had so much left to do in life."

Nineteen Eighty-Five.

Garbage cans bounced and clanked, their metal lids screeching across the pavement as sanitation workers flung them like Frisbees. The noise disturbed me from my sleep. As I strained to get up, my back wrenched, forcing my arms to lift my aching body from its awkward position.

The bed I'd fallen asleep in was gone; in its place, a green bench. And it wasn't my apartment, but McNally Park. My backpack served as a pillow and it became increasingly obvious that I'd slept in the park all night. But why?

A woman wearing Daisy Duke Shorts with rips on the back pockets and a white halter top asked if I needed assistance. I asked her the year instead.

"It's like 1985," she said, sounding more like she belonged in L.A. rather than Brooklyn.

I had made it through another year, but what I was doing in the park, unknown. With no time for small talk, I grabbed my backpack and threw it over my right shoulder. I needed to find out why I wasn't in my apartment.

Sadie's was just the place for answers, but nobody came to the door when I knocked. My grandmother's vacant house signified that everyone was at work.

I walked down the block to my apartment on Avenue T and rang the bell twice, until Mrs. Russo tore open the door.

"You!" she said, in a chiding voice. "I told you, no money, no apartment. If you can't afford rent that's your problem." The door closed in my face before I could ask for a second chance.

I remembered that I'd been fired from Bargain Town. But why hadn't I found a new job?

On cue, Sadie crossed from Avenue T to Crestwood. The child was not with her.

"Sadie!" I shouted. She turned, squinted, and waved.

"There you are!" she answered. "We've been wondering where you'd gone. Come on home with me and have a little lunch." Classic Sadie.

On the way, I learned that I had indeed been evicted from my apartment and had wandered off.

"We've been so concerned," Sadie continued. "Oh, gawd."

During the walk, Sadie complained about a drought that was plaguing Brooklyn, no rain for weeks. "It's terrible," she mentioned. "Feels like everything is stuck."

Sadie practically dragged me into the bathroom and begged me to tidy up. My face was caked with dirt, matching the unkempt clothes hanging from my body. Although a shower would have been ideal, I didn't have a change of clothes. I scrubbed my face and arms with a green washcloth while Sadie chattered through the door.

"Flo will be so happy to know you're awlright. She was worried about you. And she doesn't need the extra worry, ex-specially with Ann not feeling well. Poor Ann. I hope they find out what's wrong with her. Her stomach has been giving her a lot of grief these days. Gawd love her."

The washcloth tumbled into the sink of grimy water. It was 1985, the month I wasn't sure about, but my mother's illness did not grow overnight.

I tore open the bathroom door unable to contain my emotions. The stranger had warned that I would live through everything, even the parts I did not want to accept.

Sadie lugged her bad leg over to a chair and sat down. "Is everything awlright?" she asked.

My mother's health was in decline. She would suffer even more once the cancer metastasized to her liver and lungs, once her inflamed legs kept her from walking and her obtruding stomach condemned her to endless agony.

I couldn't stand by and watch it happen, but what could I do – go to her doctor and beg him to check her pancreas until the tumor was found?

Yes, that's what I could do. What I would do.

Dr. Philips was my mother's doctor at Parkway Medical Center. She'd seen him over a year with complaints of stomach pain and swollen joints. But he couldn't locate the cause, so she was misdiagnosed.

I hated the doctor for giving her the wrong information, even though my father explained that pancreatic cancer was not easy to find. Most times it didn't appear until it was too late.

The information I could provide would save my mother.

I felt an incredible need to hurry as if time were running out, which it was. I stopped for directions, my memory unclear about certain venues I had not been to since my childhood.

A middle-aged man with a cigar hanging from his lips blew smoke in my face. His swollen stomach extended underneath his white shirt and slung over his pants. He said, "Two blocks up, turn left, go one block, then make an immediate right.

I circled the same block multiple times before stopping to regain control of my heart, which promised to pound its way through my chest if I didn't slow down. The vindictive universe sensed my urgency, making every step feel like I was on a treadmill, running fast but getting nowhere.

And then it appeared: PARKWAY. A line of trees bordered the sidewalk opposite the facility. I slithered through the revolving door and practically knocked over an old man with a cane, which he vehemently shook at me.

At a nurses' station, I tapped the partition until someone pitched aside the sliding window. "Can I help you?"

"I need to see Dr. Philips," I answered.

"Are you a patient?"

"No, but it's crucial that I see him right away."

"Please fill out these forms and take a seat in the waiting area. A doctor will be right with you."

"I don't want to see another doctor," I exclaimed as the clipboard hit the desk. "Get me Dr. Philips now!"

Unimpressed by my eruption, the woman's persuasive frown advised me that I was wasting her time.

"The doctor has a full day of patients," she rebuked. "You will see whoever is available. Take a seat."

The waiting room was packed with people coughing and sneezing, a young girl with her arm in a sling, and one guy with a rag held against his bleeding nose. And there I was trying to figure a way to get by the sentry to Dr. Philips with vital information on my mother. And in the process, I would inform him about my father because he was his doctor, too.

As I waited, my own doctor's visit surfaced in memory.

After my thirtieth birthday, I was feeling run down and needed bloodwork. I'd gone for my physical expecting something to be wrong with me. Nothing major, but something. John thought I was insane and Jen seconded the motion. "Do you have a death wish?" John asked. But he didn't get it, nobody did.

When my doctor declared me in perfect health, I shrugged it off. "Given your family medical history," the doctor said, "you're a lucky young lady."

I didn't feel lucky. Why had my mother been made to suffer along with my father, while I walked the earth unscathed?

A doctor emerged and handed a file to one of the nurses as she engaged in a lengthy phone conversation. "Thank you, Dr.

Philips," she said, before turning back to the phone. It was my chance to approach the doctor and plead with him to listen, but he left in a hurry.

I got to my feet and inched toward the back of the hospital. The nurse on the phone yammered away, another nurse sat with her legs crossed while she filed her fingernails. That's when I took off. My sneakers skidded off the finely polished floor; the squeal caused the nurse on the phone to release the receiver and the other to break a nail. I was midway down the corridor before they knew what happened.

Dr. Philips had gone into room 109. He held a stethoscope to an elderly woman's chest, asking her to take deep breaths. I stood in the doorway.

"Doctor," I said, "can I have a word with you?"

Philips offered a disconcerted look. "Who are you?" he asked.

"You don't know me, but I have information on two of your patients."

"I'm sorry, but I can't discuss my patients with you."

I walked into the room unmindful of the woman squeezing the back of her white dressing gown.

"Look," the doctor declared, "if you don't leave I'm going to call security."

"Please, Dr. Philips, listen to me."

The doctor picked up the phone, but I took it from his hold.

"I'm not going anywhere until you listen."

Dr. Philips glanced over my shoulder. I turned to see my mother, who, while in for a checkup, had rushed from the next room when she heard my voice.

I couldn't contain my surprise and sang out, "Mom!"

Startled by my utterance, my mother raised a hand to her mouth. All the while her eyes swam in tears. "Oh, Lynn," she said.

The stranger swayed feverishly past my mother, almost through her, to get to me. "It's over, Rebecca."

"She's my mother," I squawked until a nurse appeared and set her arm around my shoulder. The nurse didn't see the stranger. Nobody did. He was my secret.

My mother appeared jumpy, stuttering and stumbling over her words as she tried to speak. "Lynn!"

"There's something you should know," I moaned.

"Rebecca, move on," cautioned the stranger.

I hadn't planned on telling my mother the truth, but the clock ticked. Each second of her life coming closer to the last.

"You're my mother," I blurted out to everyone's astonishment. I disregarded the stranger's hands as he brought them up to his forehead.

My mother surrendered her upright position. The doctor dived for her small torso as it plunged downward.

Everyone in the room looked me over like I was in a lineup. Even the elderly woman, still clutching her gown. Their expressions identified me as a liar.

I wanted desperately to save my mother, to give life to the one who'd given life to me. But the faint whisper blared so that I could not ignore its message: *she's had enough*, it said.

I regained my arm from the nurse's grip and sped back down the corridor, straight out of the hospital. The stranger speedily behind me. I pressed through three people standing on the corner of Nostrand Avenue, unaware that I'd knocked one of them to the ground.

Flower gardens wilted as citizens fanned themselves on their stoops, hoping for a release from the unforgiving heat. Clouds loomed overhead, promising rain but delivering nothing.

I continued down Farragut Road, then hung a left on New York Avenue, then a right onto Tilden. But I could run no more upon observing an emblem mounted on a large edifice that read Holy Redeemer Cemetery.

Sixteen

The graveyard summoned me inside where the ground still thick and firm, would soon bear the remains of the most important woman in my life.

Finding the plot was no easy task, considering I hadn't been there in what seemed like another lifetime.

A mass of graves covered every inch of ground, stacked against one another like everyone belonged to one large family.

Finally, the grassy parcel of land barren of my mother's brittle frame.

I laid down and folded my hands over my stomach, imitating a body whose life had been extinguished. How did it feel being defeated by death? To lose your life before it had even begun?

There was a discreet rustling in the background. "Rebecca, it's time," the stranger said. He came from nowhere but seemed to be everywhere. I couldn't outrun him or will him away, because strangers don't leave. They wait.

My hands accelerated along the ground. I gripped the cool, smooth soil between my fingers while the stranger held out for a concession.

"I can't."

A few yards away, a black hearse pulled into the cemetery followed by a procession of limousines. Six pallbearers, leveling a casket on their shoulders, stopped at a newly dug grave. Among the throng, a girl of eleven or twelve. Her grayish expression reminiscent of someone burying a parent.

"You don't want to go through that again, do you?" the stranger asked, pointing in the direction of the little girl.

"That's why I have to save my mother." My desperate plea did little to persuade the stranger, who joined me on the ground with his back huddled against an oak tree.

"And just how do you propose to do that?"

"I was trying to inform my mother's doctor about her cancer when you barged in."

"It won't work," the stranger said.

"Oh, and you know this how?"

"Because the doctors have already run tests and the cancer isn't showing. And it won't show until it's time. You can't save your mother, Rebecca, or your father. It's not your place."

I got on my knees and practically rammed my finger in his face.

"If I can't save them, why am I here?"

"You're here because you choose to be."

"I didn't choose anything."

"You were supposed to come to Brooklyn to scatter your father's ashes. That was the plan. Once you arrived everything became familiar again, so you turned it into a homecoming instead."

"How could I have known that I would relive my childhood?"

"Oh, Rebecca, this trip didn't cause you to revert to your childhood. You've carried it with you all along."

The stranger remained composed, testing me like a criminal whose only recourse was to confess. But I was unmoved by his attempt to coerce me.

"We deserve more time. She's my mother."

That's when the stranger hit me with a blow that shook me to my core.

"She may be your mother, but she doesn't belong to you."

His severe words cut deep. Not mine? She carried me in her womb for nine months.

"Your father and your grandmother and your aunts, they don't belong to you either."

"Why do you make me suffer?" I wept, unable to sustain my tears.

The stranger got to his feet and set his hands in the pockets of his trousers.

"You suffer because of your own reluctance. If you do not move on, you will never fulfill your destiny."

A section of bark where my fingers lay began to splinter until a tiny bald spot appeared.

"What is my destiny? To be alone?"

"You're alone because you choose to be."

That word again. Choose. "As if I caused my parents to die or Jen to drop me or John to cheat on me."

"Things change, Rebecca. People change. They die. Friends move on. Boyfriends are unfair. It's all part of life, but it doesn't mean you stop living."

I used my left foot to kick a tall gravestone. "Stop living? I'm breathing, aren't I? My heart is still beating."

A sympathetic expression shone on the stranger's face. "The flesh is alive, yes, but the person inside has not lived for some time."

I was astounded by his declaration, even if I could not counter it.

"You dwell on your losses," he went on. "Every time you turn on those home movies you get stuck."

"Everyone looks at photos and home movies," I reasoned.

"Not everyone remains encapsulated in them. They're more than images to you. They bring your family to life again. That's why you never wanted to visit your mother's grave."

"That's absurd," I rebutted.

"You never accepted that your time with her was cut short. But your mother's life didn't end too soon. It's not about the amount of time you spent with her, but the quality she put into the time you had. That beautiful creature accomplished what she came to do, to bring you into this world so that you could write your own page in history. It wasn't your mother who abandoned you, Rebecca. It was you."

A tiny, plump sparrow landed on my mother's unoccupied grave. I looked at it, wondering how something so small and fragile had the courage to fly on its own.

I festered in self-pity, then plunged onto my hands and knees, pounding both fists into the earth, one after the other, like a child who couldn't have her way.

"Rebecca, you can't change the past. Can't you see how futile your efforts have been?"

"Why is it wrong to want to keep my family alive?"

"Because they're not alive. They live so long as your thoughts give life to them. But when you dwell in the past, Rebecca, you relive the same pain. Don't put yourself through it anymore. Don't put your family through it."

The mourners who had earlier come to bury their loved one had gone. The casket had been lowered. The grave filled.

"It's your turn," the stranger said. "Bury the past once and for all. Let your mother go. Let your father go. Let the child go."

I broadened my fingers against my chest. "I hate that kid!" I yelled.

"You hate yourself?"

"The child."

The stranger wandered in a circle exhibiting slow, cautious movements. "That child is you, Rebecca.

The clouds overhead darkened and resumed their threat as the stranger erected himself like a monument. I stood back without flinching, reluctant to offer a reaction.

"You sensed that your mother wouldn't be with you long, didn't you? Call it intuition. A lot of children have it. Doesn't mean that you could have prevented her death. Don't punish yourself for what's not in your control."

I looked across the cemetery, trying to get a handle on life and death. Graves every which way. Bodies beneath the ground that once lived and breathed, now stagnant. Mothers and fathers, sons and daughters, sisters and brothers. We're born knowing that death will find us, but unknowing of when. And through it all life goes on. Even without us.

My head slanted to examine the sky. "She never even said goodbye."

The stranger dropped to his knees, his arms cradling my shoulders. "Of course she did. The morning her soul lifted from her weary body while you slept, she kissed you on the forehead and whispered, 'I'm always with you.'"

"What happens if I choose to stay?" I asked.

The stranger clicked his right foot off a tree to loosen grains of dirt embedded in the sole of his shoe.

"Then you will forever look back to yesterday."

"Can I have a few minutes to go back to the neighborhood? Just once last time?" I asked.

"Whatever it takes to make peace with your past. As long as you come back here and bury it."

"This is way too hard."

He situated himself behind a tree. Another of his disappearing acts. Yet in the distance came the words, "You were never meant to save your mother, Rebecca. Only yourself."

The collar of my shirt wound around my neck. I yanked at it until it yielded. Pawed at my hair, and then threw a glance at the ground.

Defeat gave me one alternative. I chucked my backpack around my shoulders and headed for Crestwood Avenue, where my mother waited to be set free.

Seventeen

Uncle Albert made his way from the porch with two bottles of beer stashed under his right arm and a bowl of macaroni salad in his left hand. He spotted me and nudged his chin for me to follow him to the backyard.

Grandma guarded the food on the grill as Uncle Albert put his beers in the refrigerator. Sadie sat at the picnic table folding napkins. My father hovered over a cup of coffee, then threw his head back to drown his lungs.

In the far corner of the yard my mother rested quietly in a lawn chair, showered by streaks of sunbeams. She tried to get up when she saw me, but couldn't.

"There she is," Sadie yelled. "See, she's awlright, Flo."

Grandma used the bottom of her apron to clear the perspiration from her upper lip. "Where have you been?" she said.

"I didn't mean to cause any worry."

"Ann wants to speak with you."

Although disinclined, I knew it was time to say goodbye – this time for good.

"I was worried about you," she said after I took a seat next to her. My mother's frail body subsided into the fabric of the lawn chair, while her once olive skin, now colorless, sagged.

I deflected my eyes to the neighbor's yard where red and white roses bloomed through a wire fence.

"I think it would be best if I left Brooklyn."

It would have suited me to have my mother beg me to stay. She didn't.

"It's for the best."

I crossed my legs and tried to look relaxed, but my twisted body tensed. Over by the grill, a stray cat my uncles called Tiger, buffed his grey fur against Uncle Albert's leg, provoking him to release bits of sausage. My mother smiled through her agony and picked up the conversation.

"Honey, about what you said at the hospital when you called me mom. I need you to understand that I can't be here for you the way you wish I could."

"Why not?"

She sat up and swung her left leg over her right, her arms curled around her stomach, signaling discomfort.

"Because you can't spend your life stuck in reverse."

Mom's words punctured my ego. I'd been hoping to change the past when it was me who needed to change.

"There's just so much left undone," I disclosed.

Pulling me closer my mother said, "You can't worry about that anymore."

I struggled for something to say but came up with nothing. My mother huddled me in her arms and eased my words to the surface. "Say what's on your mind."

"She had no right to…"

"Finish it. She had no right to what?"

"To leave me like that. I mean, I was just a kid. When I think about all the times I cried out for her, hoping she'd find her way back and tell me everything was OK. I waited and waited and waited. Whenever she got sick, she promised she'd be fine. If she had to work late, she promised she'd be back. She always got better and she always came home. But that day, that horrible day in the hospital when she called me over to her bedside and told me she was dying. I begged her not to leave. Please, don't leave me, Mommy, please!"

Everyone in the backyard stopped what they were doing and looked over at the thirty-three-year-old going on nine. There was so much I needed to say and never could. So much my mother needed to say. Or perhaps, she'd always tried to say it, but I hadn't listened.

"Oh, honey, she never meant to leave you. It wasn't her choice. She loved you more than the entire world, her little girl. You can't imagine how hard it was for her to look into those small blue eyes and try to explain that she wasn't going to get better. Oh, if you only knew how she dreaded telling you.

My mother reached into the pocket of her shorts to pull out a tissue, which she used to dry not my tears but her own.

She continued: "I know how difficult it's been for you. The lonely days you spent wondering what you'd done wrong, like her death was some kind of punishment. You've got to let all that go and be the woman she always dreamed you'd be."

"I don't know what she wanted for me."

"Live life to the fullest, that's what. Do all the things she never could. And there's one other thing she needs from you."

"What?"

"Forgiveness."

That word – forgiveness - it struck my ears like a blade. Had I been angry at my mother for dying? The answer initiated my guilt. Yes, I blamed her for leaving. No, for dying. She died.

"I guess I've been carrying around this anger for a long time," I admitted. "But I never meant to blame her."

"Of course not."

"I forgive you, Mom. I do forgive you."

My mother smiled as though she knew me for the first time, even if I couldn't be sure.

"Death is a funny thing," she replied, trying to regain composure. "Everyone thinks if you can't see or hear, nothing's real. But it's not so. We're all still connected in the end."

"How can you be sure?"

"The heart may be what keeps the human being living, but love keeps the human spirit alive forever."

Mom grunted when Grandma called us to dinner, a clue that she was not strong enough for solid food. "I'll make you a milkshake," Grandma said. It was the only thing she could keep down.

Dad's unsettled leg caused the table to vibrate. His sullen appearance hinted distress. Sadie asked if he wanted more coffee, but he requested water instead. Cup after cup, he couldn't get enough. I viewed the belt on his pants. The strip of flexible material was pulled snug around his waist, which was noticeably smaller.

My father was about to embark on an endless fight with his health, one that would keep him in contact with hospitals all of his days. The fair skin on his arms stayed intact for the time being, but would soon become tarnished with the black and blue markings of needles.

"Frank," Mom said, "our visitor has decided to return home."

Never a man of many words, Dad managed to get out what he could. "It's better to move on."

His words, like my mother's, led me to think they knew more than they were willing to share, no matter how inconceivable the notion.

"Oh, oh, we're going to miss you," Sadie added.

"That's right," Grandma said, as Uncle Albert sat with his legs propped on a chair, beer drizzling down his chin. "Such a slob."

Dinner lasted longer than I'd expected or maybe that's just how it seemed, because I didn't want it to end at all.

Over my mother's shoulder the stranger came into view. I stretched my neck for a better look. Mom spiraled on the bench to see what I was looking at, and for a moment, I thought she saw him.

"Could I use the bathroom before I leave?" I asked.

"Of course," Grandma answered. "You can use the one in Frank and Ann's apartment." After my aunts left for Florida, my parents took their old apartment.

Inside, I found the child playing Pac-Man on her Atari. A paper plate with a hot dog and beans lay on a metal Smurf tray beside her. She had no idea what the coming months would bring. Or, maybe she did.

My arm accidentally brushed against a small vase on a stand by the door, causing it to tip over and frighten the child. She clenched her hands around her neck, but produced no sound, just wide-eyed panic. I realized at once that she was choking. I rushed to the child's side and held her face down on my forearm and thumped her back between her shoulder blades.

"Please," I hollered, "you can't die. There's so much left for you to do in life."

Pounding the child's back, my mind swarmed with memories of the inconsolable years that lay ahead. I felt sorry for her – for me - because somewhere inside, I was that child, still; a child who had lingered too long in a moment of time.

A grudge had caused the split between two people who belonged to one another – not me and my mother. Me and the child.

"It's not your fault," I cried as the heel of my hand pounded her back. "I forgive you. Do you hear me? I forgive you."

Forgiveness for the things I could not change; for the relationship with the mother I hardly knew. My mother's time on earth would remain with the child.

A large chunk of hot dog flew from the child's throat; a hardy cough emanated from her lungs.

I scooped her into my arms, and at first, thought she would fuss. But she stayed on in my embrace, perhaps feeling as I did, that we were no longer two but one.

The family, including Sadie, waited by the front gate to give me a proper sendoff.

"It's not easy saying goodbye," I murmured with a tremble. My mother took my chin in her hand and raised it.

"Remember," she said, "your parents are part of you. Now how can anyone who is part of you be gone?"

Somehow I knew she was right, that those we love remain even if the eyes cannot see nor the ears hear. There's an energy that flows from one person to the next that death cannot destroy. Where doubt treads, faith prevails.

I made the rounds offering hugs, careful not to embrace my mother with too much force. When I approached my father his eyes expanded. He crossed his arms to barricade himself. But my mother shot him a faint smile and he brought up his left arm and patted my back before stepping away and digging in his pocket for a lifesaver.

A curtain in the downstairs window flip-flopped. The child appeared behind a lace sheer. Her undersized hand passed up and down in front of her. I waved knowing that the road ahead would not be easy. But together we would endure.

"You better go before it gets dark," Grandma chimed in. It was just like my grandmother to worry. She would usually have people phone to say they arrived home safely. Though there would be no phone call, somehow Grandma would know.

Uncle Albert peeked out from the yard and shouted "Bye, bye," before letting out a belch.

Grandma's eyes shot heavenward. "He's such a pig."

I smoothed the creases in my pants still encrusted with dirt. "I'll never forget any of you. You mean more than I could ever explain."

Dad held my mother's arm to steady her; his own body beginning to weaken.

It was time to let my family rest once and for all.

I walked Sadie to her house one last time. "I'll be seeing you," she said.

"I'll miss you, Sadie."

"Yeah, yeah, but I'm always here."

I pointed at her house. "There?"

She took my hand and put it on my heart. "No, no. Right here."

I watched as Sadie climbed the stairs and stood at the top of her porch. My family waved from Grandma's front gate.

"Sooo long," Sadie yelled.

Before walking down Avenue S, I turned to steal a final glimpse of Sadie and my family, but they were gone. Everything was gone. The front gate underneath the trellis at Grandma's was nowhere to be seen. No white picket fence, no fruit trees, no patio. Just a brick home that I didn't recognize. All the homes had been transformed as well, even Sadie's. And the neighbors getting out of their cars, the ones on their stoops, I didn't know them, either.

I ran toward McNally Park and found the metal sliding board replaced by a plastic contraption. The swings also plastic. A sand box. A teeter-totter. The past was over.

Eighteen

I reached my mother's plot and found a flat, grey stone bearing her name and the words Beloved Wife and Mother.

Taking the urn from my backpack, I drew a few breaths and opened the top. My hand arched forward and heaps of dust dispersed over the terrain; a steady breeze carried off stray flecks.

The clouds could sustain no longer and heavy blobs of rain hunted the tears scampering down my face. Sheets of water flowed along my arms and legs; my sneakers consumed by the mud-covered earth. Tepid water streamed down my body, cleansing my life of the chains I had forged; each link belonging to someone that had been released.

I remained captivated by the serenity of the moment. A harmony that occurs after someone dies, when we become deaf and blind to the world around us; when the flesh of those we love no longer assumes their presence; when we're destroyed by anger and pain and regret, wanting so much to retain what belongs to us. Forgetting somehow that nothing does.

The baptism ended in a multicolored arc. I felt at peace for the first time in many years.

The same subway that had brought me to my past would lead me home – my real home.

Inside the station, I purchased a crisp MetroCard. Before I could slide it through the turnstile, a voice called out, "Safe travels, Rebecca."

The stranger.

"You never give up, do you?" I said in jest.

"You ready?" he asked.

"Aren't you coming to make sure I go?"

The stranger leaned in and clasped my hands until we resembled two people about to pray.

"I have faith that you'll do the right thing. Besides, I'll be there if you need me, like always. You just have to listen."

"I still don't know who you are?"

"Train's coming."

"Come on. Are you God or something?"

The stranger let out a hearty laugh. "God I am not. I've been revealing myself to you for years. You never paid attention."

He was good at cryptic messages, though I liked my answers straightforward.

"How come I never saw you before this trip?"

"Ah, Rebecca. You see what you want. It's just your way."

A flicker of lights discharged from a darkened tunnel. The breeze from the train whirled my coiled hair into a tangled mess.

I wanted more answers. Always wanted more answers. But the stranger was gone. Like my mother and father, my grandmother and aunts and Uncle Albert; McNally Park and Crestwood Avenue; Sadie and Meg and Mrs. Russo; Crawhorn's and the Cineplex; Bargain Town and Mr. Ricci.

Yet like my family, the stranger would always be with me, even if I couldn't see him, because sometimes the heart sees what the eyes do not.

When I got to the Port Authority, I looked again for the stranger. He was nowhere to be found, a sign that he believed in me. But as I climbed the steps of bus number 2 0 0 9, doubt reemerged. What would become of me once I returned to the solitary life I'd been leading?

I removed the journal from my backpack in search of the notes I had kept during my tour of the past. The pages I'd written explicit details on were blank. In my shock, the journal slipped from my fingers and fell to the floor, opening to the last page. I noticed scribbles of some kind before the book closed again. Casting my body frontward, I scooped the journal in my hands, flicking pages until the final one made an appearance. A sharp gasp managed to pass through my compressed lips, despite my clamped jaw. The message, printed in heavy, black crayon, an amateur handwriting with oversized lettering, consisted of two words: SAVE ME!

Epilogue

"It's no use going back to yesterday because I was a different person then."

—Lewis Carroll

Six months after my journey to Brooklyn, I was sitting in an uncomfortable chair in the admissions office at the local university. I searched for an exit, but fear would not win. My eyes darted left and right as I read and answered questions. The pen moved across the forms as if a familiar entity guided my hand. Along the dotted line, my signature. It was finished. Four years of my life confined to student loans. I was an English major at long last.

With my schedule for the fall semester assured, I called Jen to inform her that I'd taken her advice. I was going to college. She congratulated me until word of my major slipped, which resulted in moments of quiet on her end. "Did you hear me?" I boasted. Jen groaned as if the very thought of reading and dissecting literature was nothing more than an expensive hobby.

Her insolence was deafening, but there wasn't time to worry about what she thought, so I told her I had errands to run. She sounded displeased because she wanted to talk more. Funny how someone who'd once declared herself as *too busy* to socialize with me didn't appreciate when I used her own weapon on her.

A night job as the manager of a bookstore afforded me the prospect of moving into a new apartment, one with an extra room that could be used as a study. I packed my entire life into cardboard boxes and rented a U-Haul. It was a fresh start, a new life, where the past wasn't invited. I kept the home movies packed away. No need to see my life on a television screen. I had lived it more than once.

Along with my apartment and new job, I made friends with fellow bookworms and joined a gym. I slimmed down twenty pounds, which caught John's attention after he saw me leaving the gym one Saturday morning.

Then came phone calls where John's jealousy persevered.

He neither understood nor accepted my new life since it no longer included him. There were calls two, three times a day, begging me to give him another chance. During one call he whimpered like a baby whose pacifier had been plucked from its lips.

"Becky, we can work this out," he stated in a failed attempt to change my mind.

My involuntary yawn further agitated the situation. "John, I'm not coming back to you."

"Why not? Is there someone else?"

"Yes, I'm having a torrid affair with William Shakespeare."

The uncontrollable laughter coming from my end was not reciprocated by my male counterpart.

"That's not funny, Rebecca. Why won't you take me back?"

There was but one response.

"Oh, John, don't you know it's not healthy to live in the past!"

Acknowledgements

I'd like to thank God for setting me on the right path in life. To my beloved Aunt Anna: Thank you for helping me realize my dream of being a writer. To my best friend Mary: Thank you for believing in me as a writer. This book would not have been possible without the inspiration I gained from my parents, Barbara and Michael; my grandmother, Louise; Aunt Anna; Aunt Lorraine; and Julia. You are all in my heart and memory!

About the Author

Tara Lynn Marta was born in Brooklyn, New York and moved to Pennsylvania at age nine. She holds a B.A. in English and an M.A. in Creative Writing. In 2017, she was a freelance blogger for The American Writer's Museum and a book reviewer for At the Inkwell. Although she has enjoyed success as a fiction writer, she also dabbles in nonfiction and has had several pieces published both online and in print. Most recently, Tara's essay "The Dream Lives On" was published by *Blind Faith Books* in the anthology *I AM STRENGTH: True Stories of Everyday Superwomen.* She has done readings of her work in New York and Pennsylvania. She serves on the Scranton Reads Committee and has moderated several book discussions for local libraries. An avid reader, Tara enjoys classic and contemporary literature. In her spare time she enjoys hiking, biking, kayaking, and traveling. She currently works as a substitute teacher.